"I'VE ALWAYS THOUGHT YOU WERE A REMARKABLE WOMAN."

...Wykeham grinned. "Would you show me what you're doing?"

I hesitated, and Wykeham caught it. "If you'd rather not, I understand."

"It isn't that," I said. "It's just that I'm rather defensive about this. Most people don't think digging for artifacts is suitable work for a woman to do."

He looked at me gravely. "I assure you I'm not one of them."

I looked right into those turquoise eyes. They were looking right through me and I caught my breath. "I'd love to show you," I said, reaching for his hand to help him over the piles of dirt. He took my fingers in a warm clasp.

Suddenly I felt quite giddy. It was a very pleasant sensation. He kept looking at me and I felt myself being drawn to him. I leaned a little closer to him, and it seemed to me that he moved toward me...

AN INFAMOUS FIASCO

Susan Michaels

WARNER BOOKS

A Warner Communications Company

WARNER BOOKS EDITION

Cover design by Andrew Newman
Cover art by Nick Caruso

Warner Books, Inc.
666 Fifth Avenue
New York, N.Y 10103

 A Warner Communications Company

Printed in the United States of America

First Printing: November, 1989

10 9 8 7 6 5 4 3 2 1

To my mother and father
because of everything;

To Joelle just because
she's perfect.

Chapter 1

It had become my habit to carry my pistol with me whenever I went out to supervise at the digs. I had protested quite vigorously at first, but poachers had become such a scourge to the nearby estates, and there was constant mention of smugglers and spies from France, that I decided to carry the pistol solely to keep Papa from nagging me beyond endurance. Actually, he would have preferred to have me carry a rifle—he had presented me with a superb Jaeger from Germany on my twenty-third birthday—but I found it much too cumbersome. Papa thought it would be quite what I needed, and indeed, it was a beautiful piece—extremely accurate even at distances, and beautifully engraved—but it was almost as tall as I, weighed almost a stone, and gave me quite a kick when I fired it. In truth, it bruised my shoulder quite badly, but I would never have let Papa know his gift wasn't suitable. Instead, I hedged around the truth and told him I was afraid I would scratch it and preferred to carry my old pistol.

Papa has been dead for more than a year, but I still carry the pistol, more out of habit now than anything. To be quite truthful, I have never seen either a poacher or one of Napoleon's spies, but the pistol is quite convenient to brandish occasionally. It contributes well to my growing reputation for eccentricity in the neighborhood—one I nourish quite carefully. I have found that the locals tend to leave me alone, and the strangest behavior is considered normal when one is thought to be somewhat eccentric. However, as Lady Frances Martin, eldest daughter of the late earl of Wykeham, I'm extremely careful not to let my notoriety get out of hand—I prefer to leave my reputation in the country when I journey to London. I have enough trouble with the

1

ton, as I am erroneously considered something of a blue-stocking, simply because my particular interest—archaeology—is not deemed suitable for a lady of good breeding. I have regularly pointed out to my friends that since digging for artifacts of past civilizations is considered extremely suitable for a male, so it also should be for a female, but they fail to understand my position. They usually counter with some idiocy about the fact that chasing petticoats is also a suitable occupation for a male, and there should be a division of the sexes. I usually ignore such remarks; I learned long ago to follow my own instincts.

I was fortunate in that Papa allowed me free rein. He was terribly busy throughout his life trying to beget an heir for Foxcroft and the title. To this end, he went through three wives and sired a total of ten children. Of these, four were the long-prayed-for males who, much to Papa's chagrin, died shortly after their respective births. The other six of us were female, and we have always been quite healthy. There were myself, the eldest and almost five and twenty; followed by Elizabeth—or Lizzie, as we called her—although she is now quite married and refuses to be called anything except Lady Bassworth; Jane, a child of my father's second marriage, who is now nineteen and who was forced, because we were in mourning for Uncle George, to cut back stringently on the sumptuous nuptials she had planned. She was not too happy about that, but Papa insisted. Jane very quietly became Lady Avendale almost a year and a half ago. The next sisters are Barbara, or Babs, also of Papa's second marriage, who is now fifteen and fancies herself at least thirty and grown; Annie, of my father's third attempt at matrimony, who is nine and a perfect angel; and Sophoronia, who is six and has mercifully renamed herself Charlie, after our head groom, whom she much admires since he gave her an Irish setter puppy.

After Charlie's birth and the subsequent death of our stepmamma, poor Papa seemed to give up his quest for an heir and settled on having his younger brother, George, succeed to the lands and title. Unfortunately, George and his wife were drowned in a boating accident about a year before Papa's death. That left only Papa's youngest brother, Thomas, who had been quite happily blessed with two sons. Papa was very careful to write Thomas on a regular basis with advice about taking care of his sons, because the next in line was an American, to whom Papa frequently referred as "that damned rebel whelp." The rebel whelp was the son of one of Papa's distant cousins who had emigrated to the Colonies under some kind of cloud, and had lived and died there. Much to Papa's complete disgust, he had lived to a prosperous middle age, and before his death, he had managed to father five or six sons who were evidently somewhat active in American politics.

As Papa's amanuensis, I wrote Uncle Thomas almost weekly about the care and feeding of his family, always including one of Papa's dire warnings about the age and sanctity of the title of the earl of Wykeham. Papa usually ended each letter by including a litany of the horrible things that would ensue if the title and Foxcroft ever went to the damned rebel whelp.

My poor sister Jane had the ill fortune to set her wedding date during one of the worst snowstorms on record—a sudden late-spring storm that caught many of the wedding guests unprepared. Thomas was one of those who had a very precipitous journey home with his family. Shortly thereafter, he sent word that he and the boys had caught some putrid fever, and that they were quite ill. Papa was quite cut up about it. He spent a day or so muttering dire imprecations against the rebel whelp and his damnable offspring, then took no chances. He went in person to supervise the recovery of his chances to keep the title in English hands. Instead, both children died, as did Uncle Thomas, and poor Papa came home with a severe case of the grippe. I've never been sure if it was the grippe or the certainty that the rebel whelp would succeed him as earl of Wykeham, but Papa lost the will to go on.

As was proper, we buried Papa with much ceremony, notified the rebel whelp that he was now the earl of Wykeham, and settled down to wait. I gathered up the girls who remained at home—Babs, Annie, and Charlie—and we moved to the Dower House while we waited. I wanted to be settled in quite well before the new earl made his appearance. I felt it would be much easier for me to hold some authority if I were in my own establishment, and I felt sure that the new earl would not care about so small a building as the Dower House. Besides, I much preferred living there, as it was smaller, warmer, and, most important, somewhat closer to my digs.

The digs worried me greatly. It was on this matter that I felt I might have a dust-up with the new earl. He might not understand the importance of my work. At the present, I was excavating in the west field, where I had had the good fortune to unearth some bits of Roman mosaic. I knew—I simply felt it in my bones—that there were some splendid Roman ruins, certainly a villa, to be found there if I only had the time and the manpower.

I also had a running battle with Pembroke, the bailiff. He was constantly wanting to plant my excavations in turnips. On the west field, we had finally reached an amiable compromise: this year I excavated the upper half, he planted turnips in the lower. Next year we would reverse. I thought it quite lenient on my part, but Pembroke didn't see it that way. I was afraid he would convince the damned rebel whelp to plow under the whole field and shift to cabbages. He had threatened such a drastic course often enough, knowing full well the difficulty I would encounter in working amid the stench of rotting cabbages. Pembroke had absolutely no feeling whatsoever for either the acquisition of knowledge or for the arts.

I was out at the digs one particularly fine day about a year after Papa's death. It was well into spring, and digging was difficult because of the sudden showers. We—that is, our footman, Griggins, and I—had decided to try a trench parallel to Pembroke's top row of turnips. We were busy clearing away some dirt from what appeared to be a quite excellent fragment of Roman bronze when Annie ran up. "He's here, Frankie!"

I was thoroughly puzzled. "Napoleon has invaded?" I asked. If that was the case, there was not a moment to be lost—my mosaics must be covered up. It would never do for the French to find them. Everyone knew how rapacious the

French were when it came to the acquisition of artifacts.

"No, silly. Him—the earl." Annie was thoroughly exasperated with me.

"That's very nice, Annie," I said with relief, returning to my battered piece of bronze. It was about two inches square and I rather thought it might have been a small fragment of a helmet. "After all," I told her, "it has been quite a year since we notified him he was the earl of Wykeham. It's about time he showed up." I paused and stared at her, then wiped the dirt from my hands and clothing. "Is he at the Dower House?"

She shook her head. "No, we've not seen him yet. When Babs went into the village this morning, she heard he was at Foxcroft manor and had been for several days. She had just gotten home with the news when we received this card." Annie handed me what had once been quite an elegant card, but had obviously been handled by everyone at the Dower House, from Babs right on down to the grooms. It had almost as much dirt on it as my fragment of bronze.

"I assume everyone has read this," I said with sarcasm that completely missed Annie.

"Oh, yes," she gushed, "and it's the nicest note. Babs heard in the village that he's quite handsome, as well. Aren't we lucky, Frankie?"

I took the note by two fingers, noting that they weren't any more soiled than the card. "I scarcely see how we're lucky, Annie. After all, *he* is earl of Wykeham, and we're totally dependent on him under the terms of Papa's will. We would be better to hope he knows enough to provide amply for us, then go away and leave us alone."

Evidently, Annie's idea of the "nicest note" and mine were quite different. It was in careful script, but straight to the point:

My Dear Lady Frances, I am now at Foxcroft Manor and wish to see you on matters of business as soon as possible. Please let me know whether you wish to come to Foxcroft or prefer me to wait on you at the Dower House. I remain, etc., Jefferson Martin.

I handed it back to Annie. "All the warmth and charm of a lump of granite," I muttered. "The nerve of the man."

"What?" Annie asked. "Are you going to invite him to supper, Frankie? What about a dinner or a ball?"

"No such thing," I said promptly. "I don't intend to invite him anywhere. As for now, you're going back to the house, I'm going to finish up here today, and then, when I have time, I'll pen Lord Martin a note telling him I'll be delighted to come to the manor at his convenience."

"That's all?" Annie was completely stricken.

"That's all," I said firmly. "We'll make no social moves until and unless he wishes it. After all, he's an American, and we don't know how he'll receive us. Above all, we don't want to push ourselves on him. I'm sure customs and manners are much different over there."

It took no little persuasion, but I finally got Annie on her way back to the Dower House, and then I summoned Griggins to assist me. I wanted to get as much as possible done on my excavations before the new earl found out what I was doing. I was quite sure Pembroke had been at the man's doorstep the second he heard the earl was in residence. If there were not to be cabbages in my field within a matter of weeks, I would have to be firm.

Griggins and I did very well the remainder of the afternoon, and I had my piece of bronze, as well as a few chips of mosaic to bring back home. These days are quite exhilarating. The bad ones are when I turn up absolutely nothing. Last year, I dug up the entire apple orchard and found nothing of consequence except a few unidentifiable metal lumps. I didn't say so, but I secretly thought they were bits of horse harness left over from grandfather plowing and planting the trees. Of course, it didn't help at all that Pembroke was following right behind me, filling in all the holes and cursing Griggins.

I had scarcely reached the Dower House when Babs ran out. "Frankie, what do you think?" She was completely breathless and her hair, practically unmanageable at the best of times, was flying all about her face. Unfortunately, Babs inherited her mother's frizzy, wild red hair.

"I think perhaps I'm on the right track this time. Griggins

and I did unearth a few chips of mosaic today, and I believe there's more underneath that field—perhaps even the remains of a villa.'' I was quite elated over my find.

Babs, however, was not. "Not that old rubbish, Frankie. Who cares about that? What do you think of the note—the earl?''

I sighed. "Babs, your entire education has evidently been wasted. You *must* learn to speak in complete sentences. As to the earl, I think it's about time he deigned to come to Foxcroft Manor. After all, the house has been vacant for almost a year now.''

"But Frankie, what did you think of the note?'' I started for the house, Babs skipping along beside me.

I reflected briefly. "I trust it wasn't soiled when we received it, but other than that, I thought the man wrote a very fine hand, although the tops of his letters were somewhat spiky.''

Babs stopped. "You're impossible, Frankie! You know that I've been *dying* to go to London, and you won't hear of it because you can't dig in the dirt there. Now the only exciting thing to ever happen in my life occurs and you completely ignore it! Admit it, Frankie! Admit it! You're planning to ruin my life!''

"Nonsense,'' I said, stepping around her and heading for the door. Unfortunately, Babs has also inherited a talent for dramatics from some source—certainly not her poor mother. As I recollect, father's second wife, Miss Eugenia Campbell of the Edinburgh Campbells, was meek and mild beyond belief. There must have been an actress somewhere in her background, however, as Babs has always had a leaning for the melodramatic, and to my knowledge has never passed up an opportunity to play a part. She put on a fine performance this time, screeching and running quite dramatically indoors, then making a resounding crash with the door as she slammed it behind her. Jervis looked at me quizzically as he opened the door to admit me. I bit my tongue and resolved to take Mademoiselle DeSalle quite to task over Lady Barbara's lack of manners.

Unfortunately, at that moment, Griggins dropped my wonderful mosaic chips and scattered some dirt on the floor, so I had to stop and placate Jervis. He's quite particular about the condition of the entrance hall—he regards it as his particular domain. And, like most men, he does not at all approve of my avocation.

Later, when I went upstairs to see the girls, they were in a complete dither. Babs had evidently informed them that I was turning the Dower House into a nunnery, and they would never be allowed out into polite society again. Annie ran up to me immediately and clutched at my skirts. "Say it isn't so, Frankie!" she wailed.

"What?" I asked, totally at a loss.

Mademoiselle DeSalle dabbed at her eyes. She was quite an accomplished performer herself. The woman was going to have to go. I could already detect Babs simpering in the same affected French manner. "Oh, milady!" the governess wailed against a chorus of moans from Annie and Charlie. "Pleeze reconsider. The girls have need of balls and clothes and ribbons and meeting eligible young men. Zey will never do this if you do not relent!" Here she burst into a full-fledged torrent of weeping, managing to incite Babs, Annie, and Charlie to follow. The only thing not howling in that room besides myself was Charlie's puppy, which had the good sense to crawl under a chair.

"Mademoiselle DeSalle!" I yelled over the din. "You forget yourself!"

The woman looked up from her lace handkerchief and I could have sworn her eyes were bone dry. "*Oui*, milady," she said, dabbing at her eyes again. I looked at her and then at the children, who were drying their eyes. Babs looked frightful—she had really been crying, and poor Babs doesn't cry well at all: she had bleary eyes and a red, drippy nose, not to mention red splotches all over her skin. I made a note to advise her to learn some other method of getting her way.

I waited a moment for everyone to become calm. "Now, may I ask what might be the cause of all this nonsense?"

Babs looked at me defiantly. "I told them what you said."

"And that was . . . ?"

"That we wouldn't go to London and you wouldn't

receive the earl." Babs began acting like a watering pot again.

"Hush that this instant," I warned her. "You know perfectly well that I said no such thing." I stood and glared at them until there was nothing to be heard except a few sniffles. "Now," I continued, "I want all of you to remember that this man is the new earl and we're going to treat him as such. That means that we're not going to force ourselves on him. After all, he is a damn—" I caught myself just in time. "He's an American, and his manners and customs are quite different from ours. We'll be gracious, but we'll also give him time to become accustomed to us. Do I make myself clear?"

I looked from one to the other, waiting for nods of acknowledgment. I got one from everyone except Babs.

"We'll be courteous and civil, and if he asks us over to Foxcroft Manor, we'll go. If we think the earl wishes to further our acquaintance, we'll also ask him here." I paused for effect. "I think that's all, and I don't wish to hear any more of these artificial hysterics." I turned to Mademoiselle DeSalle. "Mademoiselle, I would think that you would be able to manage your charges so that incidents such as this one could be avoided. Perhaps we should discuss this later in the library."

"*Oui*, Lady Frances." Mademoiselle DeSalle looked suitably contrite as I left the room.

Later, at supper, I was agreeably surprised. It was quite an animated affair. Evidently, the girls had decided their lives would go on much as before, and were chatting happily. I noticed the new earl was not mentioned over fifteen or twenty times. I did manage to tell them about my wonderful find of the bronze fragment and the mosaic chips, but only Charlie seemed as elated as I. I can always count on Charlie.

After supper, I retired to the library to do some research. Papa had several books on early history that I had brought with me from Foxcroft Manor. I didn't really think the new earl would mind—it was highly unlikely that an American would be interested in Roman Britain. I was looking for clues about the early Roman settlements. I had found references to a few villas in the vicinity, and I had only to pinpoint the references to know where and what my mosaic was and maybe even who had inhabited the villa. It was an exciting thought.

After about an hour, I was interrupted. I had forgotten that I had requested Mademoiselle DeSalle to present herself. She looked quite young, although I knew for a fact that she was past thirty, and she made a practice of affecting gestures that were more suitable for an ingénue of seventeen. Now she sat down across from me, daintily waving her handkerchief. "You wish to discuss the lessons wiz me, Lady Frances?"

"No, Mademoiselle. The lessons are proceeding quite well." That was the rub—the woman was excellent at lessons. Even Charlie had learned the rudiments of needlework and French, while Babs had become quite accomplished on the harpsichord. I pondered briefly how to express myself, and decided that the best course was complete honesty. "Actually, Mademoiselle, I have been somewhat worried that the girls—especially Babs—are acquiring values that are not . . ." I paused, groping for a word. "That do not further their educations," I finished lamely. That was not really what I had wished to say.

"But, Lady Frances, they need to learn about being young ladies if they are to marry well."

"That is perfectly true, Mademoiselle, but Charlie is only six and Annie not even ten. They're somewhat young to be worried about ribbons and balls and young men."

Mademoiselle DeSalle nodded her head vigorously. "So true, Lady Frances, but you must think also about Lady Barbara. It is time for her to marry."

"Are you quite mad? Babs is only fifteen!"

"*Oui,* Lady Frances, but how many young ladies are married at fifteen? Besides, she will be sixteen next month, true?"

"True, but what you're saying is stuff and nonsense," I snapped. "Babs is far too young. Lizzie didn't marry until she was nineteen, and Jane was past seventeen. As for me—" I stopped, aware of the pitying look in Mademoiselle DeSalle's eyes.

"*Oui*, Lady Frances. I am so sorry for your situation. Perhaps you will someday marry that handsome gentleman your father picked for you, *n'est-ce pas*?"

I felt myself go scarlet. I hadn't realized that that particular period of my life had become servants' gossip. "I shall marry if and when I decide to do so," I said rather shortly. "In the meantime, Mademoiselle, I prefer that you concentrate on the girls' lessons and omit references to balls and young men."

Nodding an agreement that both of us knew she had no intention of keeping, Mademoiselle DeSalle simpered and pranced out of the library. After she was gone, I leaned back heavily in Papa's big desk chair I had brought with me from Foxcroft. Mademoiselle's reference to the handsome gentleman my father had picked out for me had rankled. Was I still madly in love with Harry Apsley? I hadn't thought very much about him in several years, and even before that, he had been. . . . I preferred not to think of it. After all, I had been very young. It seemed almost as if I had been someone else all those years ago when I had first met Harry.

Harry's father, the earl of Mountnorris, and Papa had been best friends when they were young. Harry was a little older than I—three years to be exact—so he was eight and twenty now, but he had been in the islands of the Caribbean since he was twenty. The last I had heard, some chit Harry had once spurned in London had happily informed me that Harry had formed a serious attachment with the daughter of a rice planter in Bermuda. I hadn't seen him in eight years.

It didn't seem such a long time, but it was. He had been so dashingly handsome when we had first met. I had been fifteen. Babs was fifteen now, almost sixteen, I mused, and I thought of her as a child. But when I had been fifteen, I had thought of myself as all grown up. Harry had been eighteen then. Our fathers had brought us together at a house party to see how we would rub together. They needn't have worried—I fell madly in love with him at first sight. Looking back, I think my feelings were a combination of doing what Papa expected of me and the influence of the rather torrid novels I was fond of at the time.

At any rate, we saw each other frequently, and the

betrothal more or less became an agreement between Papa and the earl of Mountnorris. However, both sets of parents judged us much too young for marriage, so Harry decided to sail to the islands of the West Indies for adventure before he married. I had heard, both then and later, that there was much more to Harry's hurried departure than a craving for adventure, but I was too head over heels in love to credit such tales. Besides, I saw myself as something of a heroine, waiting through adversity for her hero to return from the wars, or whatever. At any rate, Harry sailed away to Bermuda or Jamaica or some such place, and I was completely devastated for probably three or four weeks. After a short period when I swore I was dying of love, I came to my senses, immersed myself in the history of early Britain, and developed a passion for archaeology. After that initial few weeks, I doubted seriously if either Harry or I had ever thought very much of each other or of the agreed-on nuptials. Harry had, however, been an excellent excuse for me to forgo the fripperies and strictures of a London season, a proceeding in which I had not a whit of interest. I preferred to stay home, as that year I had begun digging near the old chapel, hoping to find some Norman artifacts. I did find a few very fine coins, and that intensified my desire for archaeology. Everyone in London thought I was wearing the willow for Harry, but in truth, I seldom thought about him at all. I couldn't even remember how he looked. He had been extraordinarily handsome, with dark hair and eyes, but that was all I could remember, although I could readily recall his charming smile.

I rose and turned from the desk with a sigh, carefully putting away my parchment. I supposed it was time to declare myself a spinster, to don a lace cap or be thought of by the *ton* as an ape leader. Actually, the prospect was not at all displeasing. I also supposed that I should have to write Harry and tell him—not that I had any illusions that Harry cared one way or the other now. I had not heard from him since he was two and twenty—six years ago. His letter was full of his adventures—omitting, of course, those involving the daughter of the rice planter. I had seen Harry's father in London once and asked after him, but his father informed me that he had not heard from the scapegrace in years, and was planning to send him word to return home. As that had been two years ago, I suspected that Mountnorris's demand had fallen on deaf ears, if, indeed, it had fallen on any ears at all.

Still, propriety decreed that I should write and tell Harry the betrothal had ended. I smiled to myself as I imagined the reaction of the rice planter's daughter to my news.

I went to bed, mentally penning a short note in my head. Knowing Harry, I felt sure he would prefer a touch of humor.

Chapter 2

I rose at my customary early hour the next morning and sent for Griggins.

"We'll leave as soon as the grass is dry," I informed him. "I suspect the new earl will visit us within a matter of days, and I wish to get in as much digging as possible before he discovers my project."

Griggins stood there, first on one foot, then on the other. Such odd behavior might puzzle others, but Griggins has been in the family for years, and I immediately recognized it as a signal that he had something to say. "Out with it, Griggins," I said to make his speech easier for him. Griggins has always had an annoying habit of beating around the bush, taking half an hour to make a five-minute speech.

"Do you think it's wise, milady?"

"Wise? Whatever can you be saying, Griggins? This is certainly the best thing to do. I'm not going behind the earl's back or anything—or, at any rate, not very much. I'm just trying to get in as much digging as possible. Actually, I'm afraid Pembroke will convince the earl to plant cabbages on our digs before I can get to him. Therefore, I think we should hurry and get as much excavated as possible."

Griggins looked slightly bewildered. "No, not that, milady. I just wondered if you think going out today is the wise thing to do, in view of the wild stories going about."

I had about reached the limits of my patience. "Griggins, I wish you would please explain yourself. What wild stories?"

"All those about the French spies."

"Griggins!" I was practically shrieking. "Will you get to the point! What French spies."

He shifted from his left foot to his right. "Well, the vicar's maid told Katie that Squire Stines had told the vicar to be on the lookout for some French spies that were coming about. You know how the squire is, Lady Frances."

I breathed a sigh of relief. "Yes, Griggins. Unfortunately, I do know how Squire Stines is. Since the moment we were warned to watch for any untoward French activity, the poor man has seen a French spy behind every tree." I started for the breakfast room. "I can assure you we'll be perfectly safe, Griggins. I'll have my pistol with me in case we see one of the dreaded French." I turned and headed for the breakfast room. "We'll leave as soon as I've eaten." I glared at him to quell his gloomy response. "Please have everything ready."

Griggins glared back, but he's much too well trained to say what he wanted to say. "Very well, milady," he said, turning. I politely ignored his mutterings as he went out to prepare our shovels and sieves.

It was a glorious morning. I stopped, took a deep breath of the morning fog, and looked up where the sun would be in a few hours. "It's going to be a perfect day, Griggins. I can feel it in my bones."

"It's going to rain," he said glumly, picking up some of my screens and a shovel. Griggins does not approve of my avocation either. I suspect he and Jervis often discuss it over a pint of ale. "Do you want me to take the Jaeger, in case we see a spy?" he asked as he looked at me slyly.

I picked up my share of the load. I make it a point of pride to lead the way and carry part of my equipment. "We do not need the Jaeger today, Griggins," I said briskly, brooking no interference. "Come along." I purposefully led the way as he and two footmen followed behind, muttering every step of the way.

Griggins and I were both right. It did turn out to be a very profitable morning for me. We uncovered what looked like a corner of a floor, and I could discern the beginnings of a line of mosaic. I was positively elated, but was careful to go slowly so I wouldn't damage any artifacts. My mental letter to Harry had been replaced with a mental paper to the latest volume of *Archaeologicia,* outlining my find. At last! I felt quite smug and fully vindicated. Even Pembroke couldn't argue with this find, and it would be a convincing argument in my request to the earl.

Griggins was right, as well. About midafternoon, large black clouds began to form, and by around five o'clock, a rather heavy fog had begun to settle. As our day had already been long, although successful, I motioned to the footmen to cover our find with a fine layer of dirt and canvas. I never leave a dig without covering it carefully.

It started to rain—really, more of a fine mist—and I elected to go on alone to the Dower House, leaving Griggins and the others to cover the trench. I don't mind at all getting dirty, but I draw the line at becoming wet. As I walked, the rain became heavier, and I decided to take a path through the woods that was much shorter, although somewhat overgrown. I thought the trees might offer some shelter from the rain.

I had gone about halfway through the patch of woods when I was startled by a crashing and rending of the tangle of underbrush in front of me. I stopped dead in my tracks, my hand clutching the butt on my pistol. It was comforting to know it was there if there were truly any spies about. Then I chuckled to myself about my groundless fears as a large buck came down the path and stopped a short distance from me. The buck was obviously being chased, as he was a study in fear, eyes rolling and nostrils quivering. I stood very still, not wanting to add to his fear. He was a magnificent animal.

Suddenly, out of the corner of my eye, I became aware of a stealthy movement. A man carrying a rifle was slowly stalking the buck, taking care not to make a noise or movement to startle the animal.

Fear clutched at me, and I was surprised at the onset of such an emotion. I had never really been afraid of anything in my life. Was the man a poacher or a spy? A poacher seemed more likely, so my life could be forfeit if he saw me. The penalties for poaching were severe: it could even be my life or his.

It wasn't significant—poacher or spy—the man was obviously a criminal. Besides, he had no right to the earl's deer—especially so magnificent a buck. Still, I didn't want to hurt anyone. If I cried out, he would probably run away—the risk of being caught was too great. As a precaution, though, I stood very still and cocked my pistol. If I yelled at him and he thought I was unarmed, he could still shoot me. If he didn't run, he would have to shoot or risk jail or transportation.

I wouldn't want to admit it to Griggins, but I had been somewhat overconfident—I had brought my pistol, but no extra shot. I had only one bullet. If he didn't run, I would have to do something, and shooting to wound him slightly was my only option. I'm a crack shot and never miss, so I wasn't worried about doing more than giving him a slight flesh wound. I sighted down the barrel of my pistol as he took aim at the buck. Just as he was ready to pull the trigger, I cried out, "Stop!" The noise in the silence of the woods was as loud as a shot. There was instant chaos.

He swung around, startled, his rifle aimed right at me as he pulled the trigger. The roar was deafening. At the sound, the buck wheeled and went crashing off behind me, and I threw myself on the ground, pulling the trigger of my pistol as I fell.

I lay there in the wet earth for a moment, listening to the sound of the deer running farther into the forest. The air was heavy with the smell of damp earth, powder, and fear. I heard nothing else except the harsh, grating sound of my own breathing and the ceaseless patter of the rain falling. Then I gathered my wits and took a quick survey of my body.

I seemed to be scratched and there was a graze on my

cheek—whether from his shot or a limb, I didn't know. It was only slight and didn't seem to be bleeding very much. My sleeve had been torn at the shoulder and I had received a cut across the arm. All in all, I didn't think I had any injuries that wouldn't heal in a matter of days.

But what of the poacher? I groped in the underbrush for my pistol. Although my one shot had been spent, the pistol still might serve as a club if I needed a weapon. My fingers closed over it, and I sat up slowly, listening for sound of the man. I heard nothing. I rose carefully to my feet and strained my ears. Now I could hear his breathing, harsh and low, as he gasped for air.

Slowly, I approached him. I didn't know if he was badly wounded or if he might have another weapon and still be able to use it. As I got closer, I saw that I needn't have worried.

He was lying on his back, his rifle beside him. I could see the wound on the side of his chest, very low. Fortunately, there seemed little blood, but he was extremely pale. His chest was rising and falling rapidly. I went over to him and knelt, touching the wound lightly. He jerked and moaned in pain.

I bent closer and ran my fingers lightly over his coat. My hands were trembling so much that I was unable to determine how badly I had hurt him. He gasped again and tried to make a sound. I lowered my head to catch his words, but couldn't understand anything except the word *get*. He said a name I couldn't understand.

"What?" I asked him. "What? Please say something."

He tried to speak again, but could only gasp. His pallor was ghastly and I knew I had to do something quickly.

I forced myself to pull back his coat and look at the wound. His shirt was somewhat torn, but I would have to tear it further. My hands were trembling so much that this was difficult, but I finally ripped the heavy cotton and exposed the wound. I gasped when I saw it—the bullet had traveled sideways and exited, exposing the shiny whiteness of a rib.

It probably looks worse than it really is, I reassured myself. After all, the bullet wasn't lodged in the wound, and that, I understood, was a good sign. I had heard men talking about bullet wounds, and they always said that a clean wound healed quickly. The terrible gasping was, I told myself, the way men sounded when they were shot. At least, that was what I fervently hoped—I had never seen anyone who had been shot before.

I still hadn't convinced myself when I realized I would have to stop the bleeding and summon more expert help. Blood was beginning to well in the wound.

I willed myself to be calm, then ripped the remainder of the sleeve from my bodice and folded it to make a pad. I placed it as well as I could over the wound, trying my best to ignore the man's moans of pain as I touched him. I was about to search for Griggins to come help me, when I noticed the man's flesh seemed tinged with blue. I was afraid to leave him alone.

The poacher's bag of powder and shot lay beside him. I decided to fire his rifle several times to see if anyone would come. That would be much faster than going to the Dower House for help. I calculated that Griggins and the footmen should have covered the excavations by this time, and would be near the path on their way back to the house.

I loaded the rifle and fired, then reloaded and shot twice more. Surely that would bring the men searching. That accomplished, I turned my attention to the poacher once again. I had thought the pad I had made from my sleeve would hold until we could get him to shelter, but it was fairly small, and was rapidly becoming quite soaked through with blood. When I lifted it to turn it over I realized that the wound seemed to be bubbling, and a hissing sound came from it.

Without another thought, I slipped up my skirts and removed my petticoat, fumbling at the ties. The petticoat was a relatively new one, and I couldn't get it to tear. I rolled the whole thing into a large wad and placed it over the wound, pressing as hard as I dared. I could have done better if I hadn't been shaking so, but I couldn't seem to stop.

He jerked in agony and moaned again, trying to move away from the pain. I cradled his head as best I could in my lap and kept my hands against the makeshift bandage to keep the blood stanched. For the first time in years I truly prayed, asking only that Griggins would hurry.

After a moment he stilled, and his breathing seemed a little more even. As I sat there cradling his head, I studied him carefully. He certainly didn't look like the typical lowlife who usually filched game. I wondered if he might be a spy, but dismissed the notion out of hand. What would a spy be doing shooting the earl of Wykeham's deer?

He was pale, but I could see that his complexion was usually healthy and tanned, as though he spent long hours in the sun. His hair was straight and dark brown, tinged with a few strands of gray at his temple, and was longer than most men wore it—it curled down low against the nape of his neck. As best as I could judge, he was of average height, but somewhat thinner than the men I knew. His face was strong, with the cheekbones high and pronounced, and his chin was determined and straight, with a small cleft in the middle. I wondered what color his eyes were under the pale, closed lids. The eyelashes were brown, like his hair, but were long and swept darkly across his skin. He wore nondescript clothing: buff breeches, well-worn brown boots, a white shirt open at the collar, and a dark brown corduroy jacket.

I began to become uneasy as I studied him—he looked not at all like my idea of a poacher. In fact, he looked not at all like anyone I had ever seen around Foxcroft or the village. I gasped with amazement—the stories must be true. There was no other answer—I must have run into a spy.

With great relief I heard a crashing in the underbrush. I called out and was answered by a shout from Griggins.

"Here, Griggins! Over here! Send one of the men running to take the gate from the wall. We need it for a litter."

Griggins reached the clearing and stared at me a moment, then turned and yelled an order to one of the footmen. "Send the other man to Pitchley to get Dr. Watterson and tell him to meet us at Foxcroft," I said quickly, as Griggins ran back to issue the order. He returned to the clearing and started to speak, but no words came.

"I don't know who he is," I said, answering the unspoken question, "but I'm sure he'll be fine once David works on him. I've stopped the bleeding, I think." I moved a little to rest my hand, still pressing on my makeshift bandage, and looked anxiously down at the man. "I thought at first he was a poacher, but now I fear he's one of the spies the squire warned us about. I fancy he has the look of a Frenchman about him."

Griggins shook his head slowly, his eyes huge as the blood drained from his face. "No, Lady Frances, he's not one of Boney's spies. I can tell you who he is. I saw him last night when I delivered your letter to Foxcroft."

I stared at Griggins as the implication in his words sank in, and my head began to spin. "Griggins, it can't be," I said. "Surely, you're wrong."

Griggins stared at me and shook his head. "That's him," he said.

"My God, Griggins. I've shot the damned rebel whelp."

Chapter 3

Griggins and the footman put their coats on the wooden gate and gently lifted the earl onto the makeshift litter. "I think he'll be all right," I told Griggins. I told them to carry him directly to Foxcroft. It was a short journey for the doctor, and I knew I could never inflict my sisters upon a man I had just shot.

We came in a procession to the great carved doors of Foxcroft Manor, a man carrying each corner of the gate, the earl lying still on their coats with his rifle beside him, and me walking alongside, still pressing on the makeshift bandage.

Brooks, the ancient butler, tottered out onto the steps but was elbowed aside by one of the most unsavory specimens of mankind I had ever seen. He was huge, with hands like hams and a body to match. His face looked as if it had seen more than its share of fisticuffs and drink. I tried to stand between him and the earl, fearing he might hurt the earl with those huge hands.

My stand was in vain. He put his hands about my waist, picked me up like a feather doll, and set me down about a yard away, much as one would do with an errant puppy. Then he turned to the earl.

"What happened here?" he asked roughly, those huge hands moving gently over the earl's shoulder. He pulled back the coat and the wad of my petticoat and looked at the wound. "I don't think it's too bad," I said. "The bullet didn't lodge."

He glared at me as if I were an insect to be brushed away, then picked up the earl as tenderly as a baby and carried him up the steps. The rest of us followed him.

I had no thought of propriety; I was thinking only of the earl. First, I was afraid he might not get the proper attention with that man in attendance, and second, I was quite frankly afraid of such a ruffian. I told myself that Griggins and the others would see that I came to no harm, but I still dreaded confessing my part in the earl's injury. From what I had seen, this man was deeply attached to the earl.

He put the earl carefully down on his bed and checked the wound briefly again, but with a good bit of expertise. "We've sent for the local physician, David Watterson," I ventured.

"Then he'd better get here damn quick," the man growled without looking up. "I want to know what happened."

I screwed up my courage and gave him a brief description of the scene in the forest, emphasizing the fact that it had been a terrible, freakish accident.

He stared at me and flexed his fingers. I could see he was itching to have them around my neck. However, he managed to control himself. "You?" he asked in disbelief. "A mere slip of a feather-head like you? You did this? I didn't know English ladies carried pistols."

I was stung. "I have never been called a feather-head," I retorted, "and I happen to be a crack shot."

"So I see," was all he answered, as he turned his attention back to the earl. I felt myself flush with embarrassment and guilt.

There was a commotion as Dr. Watterson arrived, and I was never so glad to see anyone in my life. David was a gifted physician, but his talents were wasted here in the country. His father had always wanted David to take over Pitchley, and had sent him to school in Edinburgh to study new farming methods. David, who had been a doctor to every cat, dog, and broken-winged bird in the county since we were children, had decided to study medicine instead. He was excellent, better than any London doctor I had ever seen, but when his father died, he had felt obliged to return to Pitchley to look after his mother and two sisters. Now he spent his time farming, which he hated; tending to the sick of the community, which he loved; and complaining to me, which made him feel better, but which I hated.

All the same, I would rather have him tending to the earl than the king's own physician, and I made haste to say so to the earl's man.

The man glared fiercely at me from under bushy gray eyebrows. "I don't trust doctors of no kind," he growled. "They've killed many a good man."

Without pausing in his examination, David said, "We've saved a few now and then, as well." He put his ear to the man's chest, then turned to me.

"Is it bad?" I asked, almost choking on the words.

David moved the earl gently so the wound was more exposed. "I can't be certain, but it doesn't seem so."

"The bullet didn't lodge?"

"No." David glanced at me and smiled. "He's going to be all right. Why don't you go back to the Dower House and rest a few minutes, Frankie? We'll get Wykeham put to bed and you can come over after dinner and see how we're taking care of him." As he spoke he was taking instruments out of his bag. "I'll need lots of hot water," he told Brooks.

I still hesitated and he smiled at me again. "You look as if you could use a glass of brandy yourself."

I put my hands up to my cheeks. Now that it was over and the earl was in good hands, I did feel strange. I was actually trembling all over. I smiled back at David. "I believe I'll take the doctor's advice. I will come back later. Perhaps he'll be awake by then.''

By the time I got back to the Dower House, I had stopped trembling. I settled for tea, instead of brandy, and felt like a new person.

Then the girls discovered I was home.

"Frankie, how *could* you?" It was Babs, being melodramatic again.

"Was there blood?" Annie asked breathlessly.

"There is no need to be macabre," I said. "It was simply a very unfortunate accident. I wish it hadn't happened, but it did. We can count ourselves lucky that it wasn't worse. I believe he'll be up and around in a few days."

"Was there blood?" Annie asked again.

"Really, Annie," I remonstrated. There was no question about it—I was going to have to find a more settling influence for the schoolroom. "Yes, there was some blood, but that was to be expected. The earl is going to be fine." I pulled Charlie up on my lap and picked some dog hairs off her. "In a few weeks, we'll all probably be laughing about this."

"Mademoiselle DeSalle says it's very romantic," Annie told me.

"And a famous adventure," Babs added.

I was very stern with them. "It was nothing of the sort. It was a great misfortune that could have been a disaster. There is nothing at all adventurous or romantic about wounding someone."

"Will he still want to visit us?" Charlie asked, patting me with a grimy hand. "Mademoiselle DeSalle says—"

"Enough," I said, interrupting her. "I don't wish to hear what Mademoiselle DeSalle thinks. As for the earl, I'm sure he'll want to visit us. I plan to go see him later this evening, and I'll have more news for you than." I put Charlie on the floor. "Now, go wash up and change your clothes for dinner."

"Must I?" Charlie looked down at her grubby pinafore.

"Yes, you must. You smell like a cross between the stable and a dog."

"A stable dog," Babs said, wrinkling her nose. "Fitting."

I intervened quickly before Charlie and Babs began the usual bickering. "Enough. Now, go wash. Be sure to scrub your face and change your pinafore as well."

I changed and washed, too. Katie, my maid, fussed around me and finally talked me into wearing my sprigged muslin and letting her put matching ribbons in my hair. I hadn't realized how much a change would help. I felt as if I could put the afternoon behind me and turn my attention for a few minutes to another pressing problem—Mademoiselle DeSalle. I didn't wish to dismiss Mademoiselle—she was excellent with the lessons, and especially strict with the girls about their French and pianoforte lessons. It was her unsteady influence that bothered me. The girls needed someone older, more settled. I was looking for a person who was interested in poetry that Byron hadn't written, propriety, and household management.

As I thought of options, I remembered a letter I had received from Lizzie some weeks before. Lizzie, as Lady Bassworth, was busy setting the *ton* on its ear, and had written to complain that one of our distant relatives from Scotland had come to visit and was slowly driving her to distraction.

I hunted up Lizzie's letter and reread the passage. There were so many Edinburgh cousins that I couldn't place the woman for a few minutes, but I finally remembered. I had met Clara Conroy in Edinburgh many years ago. She was the cousin of one of my step-mothers—Barbara's mother. As I recalled, she had the same flying, frizzy red hair and pale skin as Barbara. As I read Lizzie's description of her— quiet, mannerly, literate, and not at all Lizzie's type—I decided she was just the thing to influence the girls. This would accomplish two things. I hoped the girls might learn from Miss Conroy's example. (They seemed to regard my eccentricities as an excuse for their own ill behavior.) And, if the girls were less trouble, I would have more time to work at my digs. I simply *knew* I was on the cusp of an important find. I immediately wrote a letter to Miss Conroy, candidly explaining what I expected of her—after all, one could hardly invite a guest and, once she arrived, tell her you wished her to be a governess.

We kept country hours and so I had plenty of time to visit the earl after we ate. I went upstairs to get a shawl before I walked over to Foxcroft. The nights were still quite cool.

Just as I had selected a blue cashmere, Babs came flying into my room without knocking. "Guess what?" she asked, almost prancing around.

I gave her a severe look, which had no effect whatsoever. I hoped Miss Conroy could get here quickly. Babs was getting out of hand. "Babs, I'm much too busy to guess anything," I said. "I don't care to play games right now, because I'm on my way to Foxcroft. I hope David will still be there for I want to talk to him."

"Oh, it's David, is it?" she asked archly.

"Don't be ridiculous, Babs. You know perfectly well that I've called him David since we were in leading strings."

"I wonder what your caller would think of that?"

I stared at her sharply. "What caller? Babs, will you get that silly simper off your face and tell me who's here?" I placed my shawl around my shoulders and noticed that my hair was tumbling down. I threw the shawl down on the bed and took the ribbons and pins out of my hair. Katie was going to have to pull it up again. "Whoever this visitor is, he'll have to be quick about it. I have to go to Foxcroft and make sure Wykeham is all right."

Babs looked at me, round-eyed. "I thought you said he was going to be fine."

I ran my fingers through my hair and rang for Katie. "He is, I'm sure. I simply want David to confirm it. I even imagine the earl will be awake and talking by now." I restrained the impulse to pull a face. "I really haven't time for a guest."

"I think you'll take time for this one," Babs chirped, tossing my shawl over my head so I couldn't see. "I'm not even going to tell you who it is." With that, she skipped out of the room and down the hall, laughing all the way.

Clara Conroy couldn't get here a moment too soon.

Katie came in to redress my hair. I never wear powder and paint, so my toilette is at a minimum. I would also prefer to simply pin my hair out of my way, but Katie insists on doing it and, to tell the truth, I'm glad to have her take care of it. It's long, very heavy, and a rich chestnut color. I've often threatened to have it cut so I can work outdoors without being bothered with it, but I'll never do it. I suppose if I'm vain about anything, it's my hair, although David has told me I have very fine eyes. They're large and have a somewhat green cast, which goes very well with my skin, which is a light olive—darker than is fashionable because I work so often outdoors at the digs. Katie despairs and wishes I would become pale and unhealthy-looking and fashionable. I've told her it's no use wishing—I'll never be that way.

"Very good, Katie," I said as she put the finishing touches on my hair. "You're a wizard, as usual." I picked up my shawl and hurried down to get rid of my guest so I could go on to Foxcroft before David left. Babs was waiting for me at the bottom of the stairs, and I promptly banished her upstairs to her room. She went up the steps with ill grace, and I suspected that as soon as my back was turned, she would be back down, probably listening at the door. With a sigh, I turned and ran right into Griggins. He was smiling from ear to ear.

"I understand I have a caller, Griggins," I said, watching his grin slowly turn into a smirk.

"Yes, milady. Jervis has put him in the library." His smirk faded and his face became poker stiff under my stare. I wished to ask him who was here, but refused to give him the satisfaction of telling me. "I'll be out shortly, Griggins," I said, marching toward the library with what I hoped was a regal air.

I opened the door quietly and saw a man standing near the mantel with his back to me. He was tall, with very fine shoulders that were covered with a well-fitting coat that could only have come from Weston. I closed the door behind me. "Did you wish to see me?" I inquired. "I am Lady Frances."

He turned and my heart leaped right into my throat. He smiled, and I was fifteen all over again. It was the same engaging smile I remembered from when I was a green girl and head over heels in love. A thousand images suddenly crowded into my mind—things I thought I had forgotten.

"Harry!" I gasped.

I could say no more. I sat—collapsed—into the nearest chair and stared at him. Now that he was a grown man, he looked even more handsome than I remembered. He was now eight and twenty, and, if appearance was any indication, in his prime. He was not overly tall, but was still a little above average in height, and had the well-muscled body of an outdoorsman—broad shoulders, slim waist, and well-shaped legs. His face was tanned, and his eyes still held a glint of mischief in their bright blue. Try as I would to convince myself otherwise, I felt myself instantly drawn to him. The thought and the accompanying rush of feelings overwhelmed me. I tried in vain to sort things out. In the meantime, I sat there staring at him, trying to remember to close my mouth.

Harry grinned at me, that slightly lopsided smile that I had considered so charming long ago. To my chagrin, I still did.

"So, Frankie, you recognized me. I wondered if you would."

I thoroughly embarrassed myself. I opened my mouth to speak, but no words would emerge. I tried again, and finally managed a stammer. "It's been a long time since I've seen you, Harry." I sounded like a schoolroom miss. Babs could have—and would have—done it better.

He laughed as he walked toward me. "That, my dear Lady Frances, is an understatement."

I felt myself turn red as I searched for something else to say. "Why are you here, Harry?" It sounded not at all charming, not at all the sort of thing one would say to a long absent love who had miraculously returned. In fact, it sounded a little peevish, and I tried to amend it. "I mean, I was wondering . . ." I stopped, searching for the right word.

Harry characteristically ignored my embarrassment. He chuckled at me as I felt myself turn red. "Of course. I came to see you, my dear. I've spent all these years away thinking of you, remembering your beauty and your charm, so I decided to come see you and determine if you still cherished a . . ." He paused. ". . . a feeling," he finished lamely.

"A *tendre,* you mean" I supplied automatically, not

believing a single word he spoke. After all, he evidently hadn't had feelings for me, or if he had, they had been fairly well hidden. He hadn't sent me a letter in years.

He brightened. "Exactly the right term, my dear Lady Frances. Do you still have a *tendre* for me?" His voice held a chuckle.

"Really, Harry. I thought you had more tact and address." I was becoming mortified, thinking of the way I had thrown myself at him when I was a silly young goose. Evidently Harry thought I was much the same now as I had been then, and, unfortunately, I hadn't given him any reason to think otherwise in the last few minutes.

"Ah, Frankie, I forget myself. I've thought of you so often that I feel I know you as well as I did in London all those years ago. Please accept my apologies." He smiled at me again.

Harry's smile could melt glaciers, and I must admit that it melted me. "That's quite all right."

"Do I dare ask if you've ever thought of me during these years, Frankie?" he asked quietly, his blue eyes assessing me. "There were times in Jamaica when you were the only thing I kept in mind—the only thing that made me want to return to England."

It would have been fine if he hadn't added the last. I recalled that part of Harry's reason for leaving England had been the trouble his reputation for smooth words had caused him. Even his father had despaired of him.

I gathered my wits and dismissed his handsome, smiling countenance from my mind, and tried to concentrate instead on what he was saying. "Of course I've thought of you, Harry. Any woman would remember the man who once wished to marry her; however, I think you're doing it a little too brown to claim that my image alone sustained you during all these years."

"Not at all, my love," he said, smiling again and sitting down beside me.

"Please, Harry," I said uncomfortably, "don't address me as 'your love.' After all, it's been several years since we last spoke." I glanced at him and added dryly, "As I recall, it's also been several years since I even received a letter from you.''

He looked at me sadly. ''A few years can be a lifetime for one as young and beautiful as you, Frankie,'' he intoned fatuously, ''and only the blink of an eye to someone wanting only to return to you. Are you going to make me start again at the beginning with you?''

''Harry!'' I was getting exasperated. ''Don't try that fustian on me. It might work with some simpering school-girl, but not me, not now. I don't mean to be short with you, but this is not the time for this discussion.'' I stood and gathered my shawl around me. ''I need to go to Foxcroft for a short while.''

''Yes, I heard you have a new earl. My condolences.''

''Condolences?'' I asked sharply. I wondered if Harry knew something I didn't. Surely Wykeham hadn't died. I caught my breath and held it while I waited for Harry to answer me.

''My condolences on the death of your father. I know how attached you were to him, and what a blow it must have been.'' There was a short pause. ''Especially since an American came over to succeed to the title,'' he added.

I breathed a sigh of relief. ''Thank you, Harry. Papa died over a year ago, so I'm quite reconciled. As for the new earl, I haven't spoken to him yet. He is but newly arrived.'' This was the complete truth, as far as it went. I certainly didn't want it publicly known that I went around shooting my relatives—even the distant ones. ''How did you know about the earl?'' I asked.

''I stopped in the village to inquire,'' he said easily. ''It would have been the very devil for me to run up here and try to woo you if you had a husband and half a dozen little ones dragging at your skirts. A great deal can happen in eight years, you know.'' His tone was rueful. ''Besides, I had planned on putting up at Foxcroft while I resumed— That is . . .'' He stopped and began again. ''Well, dash it all, Frankie, I'd planned to stay with your family, but now I can't.''

I laughed. ''There's a very comfortable inn in the village, or if all else fails, there's always Pitchley.''

"Pitchley!" His eyes lit up. "I'd forgotten old David! I'll go over there."

"That would be advisable," I said, rising and trying to keep a smile from my lips. David was an excellent surgeon and an avid student, but the last thing he ever wanted was company. His sisters chattered quite enough, he always said. He would be quite upset when Harry billeted himself at Pitchley, but a new face would do David a world of good.

"I don't mean to be at all rude, Harry, but I do have a very pressing errand," I said, standing beside my chair.

Ever the essence of manners, Harry took the hint. "Of course, Frankie. I didn't mean to detain you, and I certainly should have written. Please understand that I was anxious to see you and ascertain if . . ."

"If I was still available?" I finished for him.

I thought he might blush, but I was wrong. "Exactly," Harry said, not at all nonplussed. "And since you are—available, that is—I'm delighted I came on without writing. Now, if I can only convince David to put me up at Pitchley, I hope I may become a frequent visitor here."

Thoughts crowded my mind. Much as I might like to renew my acquaintance with Harry, I had to make sure the earl was recovering and I would need to visit him frequently during his convalescence. Then, there was the matter of my mosaics.

"Frankie?" For the first time since I had known him, Harry's voice seemed a trifle uncertain.

"I'm sorry, Harry," I said with a smile. "I was wool-gathering. You're welcome to come here at any time. All of us are delighted to know you're in the neighborhood."

He clasped my hand and touched it briefly with a kiss. "It's wonderful to see you, Frankie, and I want to see you again as soon as possible. We need to talk—not only about old times, but about," he paused significantly, "other things."

"Not now, please, Harry," I said firmly. To my amazement, his touch had quite unsettled me. My hand tingled where he had kissed it. I was too old for such, I reminded myself, and stepped back to put some distance between us. "I need to go."

His eyes searched my face, and I made my expression

blank. "As you wish, Frankie. I'm going over to Pitchley. I hope David isn't the same stuffy scholar he used to be."

I laughed. Harry had always had the power to charm me out of a bad mood. "Unfortunately, David is exactly the same. However, I expect if anyone can convince him to put up with a rogue for two weeks, you can."

I saw Harry out as Griggins and Jervis looked on with smirks on their faces. Men—even servants, who should know better—are completely disgusting at times. The second Harry was out and the door was closed, I turned on them. "Not a word of this to anyone," I said sharply.

"Lady Barbara welcomed Lord Apsley," Griggins pointed out.

I made a face. If Babs knew something, the entire country knew it in a matter of minutes. There was nothing to be done about that matter. Besides, Harry had been well-known in the neighborhood long ago; it wouldn't take him very long to renew acquaintances. With a sigh, I gathered my shawl around me. "Let's go, Griggins," I said. "I want to get to Foxcroft and see the earl, then get back early. Unless I miss my guess, we'll have a busy day tomorrow. I think we might even uncover a floor or part of an atrium."

"Atrium?" Griggins was completely blank.

I chuckled. "Never mind, Griggins. Did you get the barley water from cook?" As we walked, I composed the apology I intended to present with the barley water.

-------------------- **Chapter 4** --------------------

Mrs. Simms, the housekeeper, and not old Brooks, opened the door when we knocked at Foxcroft.

"Oh, Lady Frances," she wailed.

"Whatever is going on, Mrs. Simms? Why are you attending to the door? Has Brooks fallen ill?"

Mrs. Simms started sobbing again. "Oh, milady, everything's all at sixes and sevens! It's the earl's man, Perkins. I tell you, a bigger rascal I've never seen. He's made Brooks go up and nurse the earl, and what with poor Dr. Watterson doing everything he could, and then me telling them to send for you . . .'' She broke into a wail again.

"What are you saying, Mrs. Simms?'' Suddenly, there was a chill in the air and it seemed to surround my heart.

Mrs. Simms mopped at her eyes ineffectually. "They're afraid he might die—that's what. I told them I could do better in the sickroom than Brooks, and I told them to send for you. You know how you helped when the measles were all over the village. A woman knows something about nursing, you know. Brooks, indeed!''

I caught only one phrase. "Might die?'' I put my hands on her shoulders, as much to support myself as to quiet her. My knees had turned to water. "Are you talking about the earl? That's impossible, Mrs. Simms. He was doing quite well when I left for the Dower House. David told me he was going to be fine.''

"Well, he's not now,'' Mrs. Simms said, wiping her face again on her apron. "Dr. Watterson's afraid he's going to die. I heard him tell that Perkins so with my own ears.''

"Die?'' I almost choked on the word. I pushed Mrs. Simms aside and ran up the stairs, forgetting manners and everything else, except the earl. I was out of breath by the time I reached his chamber door, and had to stop and lean against it before I could bring myself to knock.

David opened the door. "Good, you're here,'' he said. "We're going to need everyone we can find.''

"David,'' I said, almost pleading, "tell me it isn't true. Please. Mrs. Simms told me that the earl might die.''

David looked down at me and took my hands in his. "I'm sorry, Frankie, but it's quite true.''

"How?'' I asked, choking back tears. "The wound looked so clean and the bullet didn't lodge. There wasn't even as much blood as I thought there would have been.''

"All that is so,'' David said, "and I know I led you to believe everything was going to be fine. I knew that the lung had been punctured by a fragment of bone from the shattered rib. I wanted you at home where you wouldn't hear me operating. His lung has collapsed, Frankie. That's why his breathing was so uneven."

"Oh, David," I sobbed, leaning into him and putting my head on his shoulder.

"Now, Frankie," he said, smoothing my hair, "don't cry. It must have been a terrible shock, coming on a wounded man in the woods. I wonder who did it?" His tone suggested that the thought had only just occurred to him; he must have been very worried by the earl's injury. "Did you see it happen?"

"I did it."

David paused and looked up at me in astonishment. "You? I thought you were a better shot than this, Frankie. What happened? Were you trying to warn him off? Did he . . . threaten you?"

"He moved unexpectedly," I mumbled, feeling my face flame with guilt. "I thought he might be a spy—or a poacher—and wanted to frighten him."

"Then it wasn't your fault."

"Do you really think that's any consolation?" I asked bitterly. "The man might die, and if he does, will it make any difference whose fault it was then?"

"You did what you could," David said.

I shook my head. "No, I didn't. I should have called out to him. I should have shot into the air. I should have done a dozen things besides what I did. If he dies, it'll be on my head. And he will be *dead*."

David grabbed me by the shoulders and shook me. "It was an accident, Frankie. There was nothing else you could do. You probably saved his life as it was, and now you can do something else for him. Stop crying, I know you're made of sterner stuff."

David was quite right. I stood tall and took a deep breath, then rubbed the tears from my eyes. "I'm surprised Perkins didn't tell you what happened."

"Him? Perkins only growls at me. Brooks and Mrs. Simms are beside themselves. I'm glad you've come. You'll be a great help."

"I'll try, David. Just tell me what you want me to do."

David knew me well enough to know that my sense of

responsibility wouldn't let wild horses drag me away this time, and that I would fret less with a task before me. "You're going to have to help us pull him through this. He has a chance, albeit a slim one, and he's going to need all of us helping him. Mrs. Simms tells me that you're an excellent nurse."

"I'd hardly use the term *excellent*," I told him. "I've helped my stepmothers in the nursery with colds and such, and you know what I did in the village last year when the measles were rampant. Those things are much different from the earl's injury. I want to help, but don't think I can do very much, David."

"Nonsense. Let's go inside. I want you to see for yourself that the earl has a fighting chance."

We went into the darkened room. I could see Brooks hovering in the background and Perkins still standing where he had been when I had left. I didn't think he had moved at all. He glared at me, and it took all my courage to stare coolly back at him. I don't think I could have done it if David hadn't been beside me.

David walked with me over to the bed, and he frowned as he looked down at his patient. Wykeham was lying quietly in his bed, the covers pulled up around his shoulders. He looked singularly handsome, but still pale. David turned back the covers and looked at his hand. I saw that the nails were bluish. The earl's breathing was ragged and uneven.

"David," I said softly, trying to keep the emotion out of my voice as I looked at Wykeham, "I fear the worst."

"I told you it was a possibility, Frankie." David's long, slender hands smoothed the covers as the earl moaned and tried to move.

"Are you sure there's even a chance?" I stared in fascination at the chiseled, high-boned face of the earl, imagining it set in death. It already looked waxen.

David looked at me, but I didn't see much hope in his eyes. "I don't know, Frankie. I truly hope so. I've done the best I can, and Perkins assures me that the man's a fighter."

"I didn't truly realize that I might have killed someone, David," I whispered, unable to keep the trembling out of my voice. "I thought that once we got him to Foxcroft, and once you got here to take care of him, everything would be all right.''

David put his arm around my shoulders, pulled me close to him, and smiled down at me. ''Let's hope it will, Frankie. Haven't we nursed many a cat, dog, and horse back to health in our time? We'll do it this time, too.'' In spite of his hopeful words, his tone was worried. I wish I could have believed him.

I put my head on his shoulder. ''Dear David,'' I murmured. It was good to have a friend.

There was a low growl from the other side of the bed, and we looked up to see Perkins staring at us warily. I immediately read his expression and realized the man thought we were in collusion to harm his beloved master. David must have read the same thing. He moved his arm from my shoulder and became very professional. ''Now, Lady Frances,'' he said briskly, ''I don't want the earl to be alone for a minute. I've decided we'll watch him in shifts, so there'll be someone here around the clock. We can take either eight-hour or four-hour shifts. There will be you and Brooks, Griggins and me, and Perkins and Mrs. Simms.''

''Very good, David,'' I said, my voice demonstrating a coolness I certainly didn't feel. ''I'll send Griggins back with a note to the Dower House and have Katie send over some clothes.''

I glanced at the earl uneasily as he shuddered and struggled for breath. ''David, I suggest the four-hour shifts, as we might tend to sleep during a longer stay.''

''I intend to stay put.'' The voice was a low, menacing rumble.

''Nonsense, Perkins,'' David said. ''Lady Frances will do a perfectly adequate job, and Brooks will be here with her. I'm sure he'll call you if you're needed.''

''I'm staying.'' He sat down in a chair near the bed, folded his arms across his chest, and stared at us with a look that dared defiance.

''Very well, Perkins,'' David said, quite practically, I thought. ''It isn't at all necessary, but you may stay if you don't interfere with the others. I expect you to be rested for your shift, however.''

"Don't worry about *me*," Perkins said, with a look at me that spoke volumes. I realized with a shock that he was staying because he fully expected me to murder his master right there in his bed. I felt my jaw drop.

I excused myself for a moment, both to compose myself and to send notes to Katie and the girls. I paced the library for several minutes, fuming over the look on Perkins's face and the implication in his words. I finally calmed down enough to realize that perhaps I would feel the same way if I were in his place, then helped myself to a small glass of brandy from the decanter and went back upstairs.

Brooks and I took the first shift, sitting under Perkins's watchful glare, while David went to Pitchley for a change of clothes and then to make his evening rounds. It wasn't until after he was gone that I remembered Harry was waiting at Pitchley for him. David would have to explain the circumstances to Harry. What a contretemps! There was no way I was going to be able to conceal this from Harry now. David would simply have to explain everything to him, and I would have to hope for the best.

Sure enough, when David returned, Harry accompanied him. "I volunteered to assist," he explained to me. "You should have told me about this, Frankie, darling. I've seen war wounds in the Caribbean, so, while I'm no nurse, I can lend a hand."

I was in such an agony of embarrassment that the "Frankie, darling" slipped by me. "Did David explain what happened?" I asked, without meeting Harry's eyes.

Harry took my hand in his. "Of course he did, Frankie, and there's no reason for you to worry. I have enough conduct to know not to spread tales like this. Besides, it was an honest mistake. We all know that the daughter of the earl of Wykeham doesn't go around the forest looking to shoot her father's heir." I looked up at him as he smiled at me—that quirky, lopsided smile that had always brought me out of the doldrums. "I'm sure the earl will forgive you when he recovers."

The charm of Harry's smile didn't work this time. "He may not recover, Harry. David says there's a real chance that he might die. His lung has collapsed, and there's a possibility that he might get a fever. It was raining when I shot him, and he was thoroughly soaked. There was dirt on the forest floor—and so much blood. He's cold when I touch him." I tried to hold back my sobs, but couldn't.

Harry reached over and wiped my tears with his fingers. "Frankie, hush that nonsense." He sounded his usual cheerful self. "I'm sure he'll recover. I've heard these Americans are indestructible. Cornwallis thought so, at any rate." He laughed as he spoke.

"Don't try to make fun, Harry." I shook my head. "I'm still afraid he might not make it. And Harry—if he dies, what will they do to me?"

Harry instantly became grave. "No one's going to harm you—not while I'm around. In the meantime, don't even think about it, Frankie. It's not going to happen."

"Will I have to go to jail?"

Harry wrinkled his forehead in thought. "It's been a while since I gave much heed to the fine details of English jurisprudence, but I believe you might get off with an inquiry. Once the circumstances were explained, you'd be acquitted, I'm sure. Any jury in the world would recognize that it was an accident." He paused a minute. "Damn the man, anyway! He should have introduced himself to you the moment he arrived. Then you would have recognized him."

"It's too late for 'should haves,' Harry."

"Don't worry, sweet." He pulled me close to him and put his arm around my shoulder. It felt very strong and comforting, and to my surprise, I completely enjoyed the sensation. It was wonderful just to melt against him and feel his arms holding me.

We were interrupted by Perkins. He looked at me with unveiled distaste, and I realized that the last time he had seen me, David had had his arm around my shoulder. Evidently Perkins thought me somewhat loose.

He ignored me and addressed Harry. "Begging pardon, Lord Apsley, but Dr. Watterson asked if you could come to the earl's chamber. He wants to give the master a draught of some kind to help keep the fever away."

Harry released me immediately. "Certainly."

Harry gave me a wink and a smile as he left, but it wasn't

very reassuring. I watched Perkins lead the way up the stairs, then found Mrs. Simms and asked which bedchamber had been prepared for me. Katie had sent me several changes of clothes and had requested that she be allowed to come to Foxcroft to dress me and to lend a hand in the sickroom, but I refused. With no one at the Dower House in charge except Mademoiselle DeSalle, I felt Katie was needed there.

"I put you in your old room, Lady Frances," Mrs. Simms said, leading me to a familiar door. When I went in, I glanced around and discovered that it didn't feel like my room anymore. I dismissed Mrs. Simms and sat on the edge of the bed, shoving aside the things Katie had sent me. I had done nothing for the past four hours, but I was completely exhausted, both in body and in spirit. I didn't ring for a maid; I didn't even put on my nightgown. I merely threw myself across the bed and did something I would have deemed impossible: I fell into a sound, dreamless sleep.

I was awakened some time later by a chambermaid knocking on the door. It took me a moment to realize where I was and why. With an effort I sat up and called for her to come in. "The earl?" I managed to ask as she slipped in the door. "Is the earl worse?"

"No, Lady Frances, I don't think there's been any change," she said, looking at me warily. "Mrs. Simms told me to bring this up," she added, putting a tray loaded with steaming dishes on the table beside the bed. She took a long look at me and dashed out the door, apparently terrified. *Surely*, I thought to myself, *I don't look that bad*. I roused myself and went over to the looking glass. My hair was a tumbled mess, and I did look the worse for wear, but hardly ghastly enough to frighten the maid. I decided she must have heard of my reputation as an eccentric. I had promoted it to a small degree, but to my annoyance, it had become embellished by the neighbors.

I hadn't thought myself hungry, but the smell of the food quickly dispelled that notion. I was ravenous. I had to force myself to eat slowly to keep from bolting my food like one of the coachmen. I was almost finished when the timid maid returned.

"Anything else, milady?" she asked, walking around the edges of the room, giving me a wide berth.

"Yes," I answered promptly. "Three things. First, come over here, please. I'm not going to do anything to you, you know." I gave her my best smile and waited until she stood in front of me. "That's better. I believe you're new here, so, second, what's your name?"

"My name is Charlotte, milady. Mrs. Simms told me to attend to you." She bobbed her head in confusion.

"Very well, Charlotte. If we're to get along well together, I want you to stop this nonsense of scampering in and out the door." I smiled at her again to reassure her.

She bobbed her head again and rolled her eyes. I thought she was going to bolt again. The girl reminded me of a very frightened rabbit. "Very good, Charlotte. Now, as to my third request—I would like a hot bath. Is that possible?"

"Oh, yes, milady. I'll see to it right away." She bobbed her head again and was out the door like a shot. In her haste, she forgot to take the empty tray.

However frightened she was, Charlotte was prompt. She immediately sent a footman up with a tub, and that was followed shortly by two men carrying steaming buckets of water. Charlotte came in to make sure the bathwater was the right temperature.

"Excellent, Charlotte," I said. "Now, will you please help me remove this gown and lay out something clean for me to wear?"

She was hesitant at first, but I made it a point to talk to her. She was from a neighboring farm and this was her first position. By the time I had bathed and she had helped me dress, she had gotten over most of her skittishness. This time, when she had the bath and water removed, she remembered to take the tray and even asked if I wanted anything else.

I felt much refreshed after my bath, so I hurried downstairs, seeking more specific news of the earl. I found Brooks, who told me that nothing had changed, and the earl still hadn't awakened or spoken, though David thought his pulse a little stronger. I went upstairs, opened the door to his chamber, and looked in. I could hear his breathing across the room, harsh and gasping. I closed the door and sagged against it. I had been hoping for a miracle, and there hadn't been one.

There was nothing I could do. David did not want the sickroom crowded, so I went to the library to wait until it was my turn to take another shift. I noted the time as I passed by the large clock in the hall and realized I had slept longer than I thought. I had only about an hour until my shift.

The library was quiet. When Papa was alive, he would sit at his large desk and work on his accounts and papers while I either served as his amanuensis or read quietly. The library had always been my favorite place in the house. It was here that I had first found the dusty, neglected manuscripts and books about early Roman days in Britain that had whetted my appetite for my avocation.

I looked around now. Already it seemed different, as if it belonged to someone else. The earl couldn't have been here over a few days, but in the short time he'd been in residence, he had already put his stamp on the room. Over the fireplace where the picture of my grandmother had been, there was now a portrait of a pretty woman with brown hair. His wife, perhaps? I had thought him unmarried, but perhaps he had wed recently. The news from America was notoriously unreliable. I wondered where she was.

Propped along the gun cabinets my father had filled with his notable collection were two or three very fine rifles. One was a Jaeger remarkably similar to my own. The others were equally well-crafted, but of a design and make unfamiliar to me. One bore a mark I did recognize—the rebel whelp had once sent Papa a rifle from America that had been made in Pennsylvania. This one had the identical mark and a long, octagonal barrel that had been rifled for accuracy in the woods. It was a frontier rifle, Papa had told me.

There was also the man's paraphernalia: bullet molds, a sizable chunk of lead, a horn of black powder, and some wadding. Evidently, the new earl enjoyed shooting and hunting. It certainly would have helped a great deal had I known that fact, I thought somewhat ruefully.

Scattered over Papa's desk were the estate account books,

with corrections and additions made in the fine copperplate I recognized from his note. He had a strange handwriting—the bottom loops were almost even and round, while the tops of his letters were straight and spiky.

I sat down in Papa's massive chair. I was a stranger here, in the house in which I had been born and brought up. Everything was familiar, but still yet unfamiliar. Even though he had been in residence but a short while, it was his house now.

I sat there, pondering over this fact and many others, not the least of which was my future. It might include marriage to Harry. It might also include a very nasty inquiry into the death of a peer of the realm, I reminded myself. Still, my thoughts kept returning to Harry. I was surprised that I still had feelings for him. I had thought that was all past in my green, girlish years. Was I still in love with him? For that matter, had I ever really been in love with him? Right now, I didn't know the answer.

After a period of unproductive thought, Charlotte came to remind me it was time for me to go to the sickroom. "Mrs. Simms sent me," she said, quavering a little but managing to stand her ground.

I gave her what I hoped was an encouraging smile. "Very good, Charlotte. Thank you."

Mrs. Simms and Perkins were just finishing up their shift as I let myself quietly in the door. I was pleased to note that Perkins was sprawled in his chair, quite sound asleep. Mrs. Simms gave him a derogatory look and sniffed. "Men are of no use in a sickroom, and don't think I haven't told him so, milady."

"Good for you, Mrs. Simms," I murmured. "How's the patient?"

"I'm truly worried about him," Mrs. Simms said, smoothing down the covers absently.

In truth, the earl looked wretched. He was still as pale as death, but he was trying to move, and every movement brought a low moan of pain.

"He's been thrashing about like that for the past hour or two," Mrs. Simms whispered. "He's felt some warmer to the touch, and I'm afraid he's starting to take a fever. I wanted to wait until you came up to see if I should wake up Dr. Watterson." She glared in Perkins's direction. "I wasn't about to ask *that man*."

"Very good, Mrs. Simms. You did exactly the right thing." I reached down to quiet the earl and put my hand on his forehead. His skin was as dry and hot as ironed parchment. I felt his cheeks and hands. They felt the same: the heat seemed almost to burn my palms. "I think Dr. Watterson should be called immediately," I said to Mrs. Simms, trying to remain calm. Actually, I was in a panic, as I remembered clearly that David had said the earl would be done for if he caught a fever.

I wet a cloth and began to sponge his face while Mrs. Simms went to fetch David. He arrived in only a moment, still struggling to tuck his shirt into his breeches. I moved to one side as he attended to his patient. His quick, sure hands checked the wound expertly.

The earl moaned and jerked suddenly, causing fresh blood to stain his bandage. David felt his head and muttered, "Damn."

"Is it bad, David?" I asked quietly.

His eyes met mine and he nodded. "It's worse than bad, Frankie. It's going to be touch and go. Are you sure you're up to it?"

"You know I am."

"Good girl. I knew I could count on you, Frankie." He moved to the table that held his bag of medicines and extracted a small bottle. "We'll have to sponge him with water and alcohol to try to keep his fever down. I'll spend this shift with you." He poured some liquid into a spoon. "We'll have to undress him to sponge him."

I felt my face flame, but managed to look steadily at David. "I know. I can do it. How long until we know something?" I asked.

"Until the fever breaks," he said, glancing at me, then added, "or until he dies."

It was one of the worst times of my life. The entire activity of the household centered on the sickroom, where the earl wavered between life and death. My existence revolved around my four-hour shift: nothing else had any real substance. I ceased to care about my appearance, merely pinning my hair up out of my way, and worried about my sisters only to the extent of sending Charlotte to the Dower House every day with messages that all was the same and I didn't know when I would be back home.

David was absolutely heroic. He only left the sickroom to attend to his other patients and had a cot brought in so he could sleep there. He took on a haggard look as he fought alongside his patient. I had never admired him more, or realized the extent of his compassion and devotion.

Harry, as well, surprised me greatly. Gone was the careless scapegrace of eight years ago. He still had his quick and ready wit, and frequently brought us out of the doldrums with a word or smile, but he also helped, just like the rest of us. He did his part without a single complaint. He stayed at Pitchley, but came over to Foxcroft every single day promptly at ten, and stayed until after midnight.

Harry had not changed completely. He did corner me once in the library early on, but I told him that I was too tired to discuss any future we might have, and at any rate, my future was tied up with the earl's. I could have no thought of anything else until I knew whether the man would live or die. To Harry's credit, he accepted this and said no more.

Perkins, true to his promise, stayed right beside the earl, almost daring anyone else to touch him. The big man was gentle as he sponged and turned the earl, and often spoke encouragingly to him.

On the fourth night of the fever, we were all worn beyond tired.

"I just don't know anything else to do, Perkins," David said as I stood by. He had finally dosed the earl with laudanum, for he was delirious and David had decided that while the opiate would hamper his breathing, his struggles might tear the internal stitches and cause bleeding in the chest cavity. I was carefully sponging his face and chest with a mixture of lavender water and alcohol. It had been agreed that I would take care of his upper body, but that Perkins or David would sponge the rest. I had argued against that. As it was, I was already past the bounds of propriety, and one more mark against my already shaky reputation couldn't signify. If anyone discovered that I had been alone in the house with David and the earl, chaperoned only by a housekeeper, my reputation was as good as gone, the earl's condition and David's engrossment in his patient notwithstanding. I didn't care at all. I didn't really care about anything except making sure that I was doing everything I could to help Wykeham's survival.

The sponging didn't seem to be helping. Wykeham was so hot that his skin warmed the cloth and the water.

Perkins looked down at his master. "Think of something else," he pleaded. "*He* wouldn't give up."

"That's true," David agreed. "A lesser man would have broken hours ago."

"Maybe you should bleed him," I suggested.

David shook his head. "I know it's the accepted practice, Frankie, but for the life of me I don't think making a man weaker is going to help."

David sent me out so he and Perkins could strip Wykeham and sponge his whole body. I was glad to leave for a few minutes for the room was hot and smelled of illness. Perkins insisted that the windows be closed, afraid his master would contract a lung disease from the outside air. I itched to open the windows and let Wykeham have one cool breath. He labored so to breathe in that hot, stale air.

I knew from experience that if I walked to the library and sat there for five minutes, I could then slip back into the earl's room. I must have fallen asleep in the library chair. The next thing I knew, Harry was shaking me gently. I opened my eyes to find him smiling at me.

"How is he?" I muttered groggily. "He hasn't . . ."

Harry knelt down in front of me. "No, there hasn't been any change—everything's just the same."

I gave a ragged sigh. "I'm about to give up, Harry. He's going to die—I know he is."

Harry stood and smiled at me again. "Don't talk like that. I've never seen you this way before."

I gave him the ghost of a smile. "Do you mean that literally?"

"Well, Frankie, I suppose I must be honest with you."

He gave me his charming, lopsided grin. "I've seen some unkempt misses in my time, but you do look the worse for wear."

I roused myself and felt the tumbled mass of my hair carelessly piled back and pinned, and made a futile attempt to smooth it. "If I look as terrible as I feel," I told him, "then I must be a fright." I straightened out my cramped limbs and grimaced.

"What you need is breakfast and a brisk walk around the grounds," he said, pulling me to my feet.

"Couldn't we at least wait until morning?"

He laughed at me. "It *is* morning, you peagoose. I just rode over from Pitchley and it's past ten o'clock. I thought you were used to country hours and early breakfasts."

"Ten o'clock?" I was horrified. "Harry, I must go back upstairs. I've slept right through the time I was supposed to watch the earl. I didn't finish helping David and Perkins; they must be exhausted."

"Everything is well in hand," he said firmly. "There's no change, and there's nothing you can do right now." He reached down and pulled me up from the chair. "You're going to eat, change your clothes, and go out for a walk with me. If you don't, *you're* going to be ill. I've already informed David that I'm taking you away for a walk. He may be the doctor, but I know enough to realize when someone needs to get away for a few minutes."

"How's Wykeham's fever? Harry, I can't get away even for a few minutes if he's no better."

Harry glanced at me. "Wipe the worried look from your face, Frankie. As I said, there's no change. He's still in a bad way and the fever hasn't broken, but David says he thinks it may be down a little. You can't do anything at all right now."

"I'm really worried about him, Harry."

"So am I, my love, but take it from one who has seen a man here and there in a fight—the man is a fighter." He pushed me through the library door. "Now, do you wish to change and comb your hair before or after breakfast?"

"Harry," I began, but he was having no arguments.

"Do you go willingly, or do I throw you over my

shoulder?" he asked with his engaging smile. "I assure you that I'm perfectly capable of doing that."

I felt the tangles around my face and looked down at my wrinkled gown, then looked at Harry and returned his smile. Already I felt better. "Before," I answered promptly.

I was halfway up the stairs to my bedchamber before it occurred to me that Harry had not only completely taken over and ordered me around this morning, but had again addressed me as "my love." The words themselves had sounded almost like a caress the way he said them. I smiled to myself as I went on up the steps. Yes, very definitely, the phrase had a nice sound to it.

Chapter 5

When I returned to the breakfast room, looking much better than when I had gone upstairs, Harry seated me and put a plate in front of me.

"There's no way I can possibly eat all of this, Harry," I protested. Then, to prove the truth of my words, I promptly proceeded to devour the entire meal. Harry had given me some eggs, grilled ham, kidneys, muffins, and two kinds of marmalade. Everything was absolutely delicious, and I ate ravenously.

"I'm glad to see you're not missish about your food," Harry said somewhat dryly as I reached for another muffin. "I can't abide simpering, languishing females."

"I've never languished in my life, Harry," I answered, somewhat miffed. "You should know that." I paused as I put more marmalade on the muffin. "However, I can assure you that I seldom eat this much for breakfast. I offer as an excuse the fact that I didn't eat anything last night."

He covered my hand with his. "I thought you hadn't, Frankie. You may not realize how you're pushing yourself, but I certainly do. The strain of worrying about Wykeham is beginning to show. You need to get away from here for an hour or so.''

"I can't."

He was decisive. "Yes, you can, and you're going to. As a matter of fact, I've already made arrangements for us to ride this morning." He put a hand up to stop my comments. "No arguments."

The idea sounded heavenly to me, but I was amazed that any man would have the temerity to *order* me to go riding. Still, I had to admit to myself that I wished to go. "Harry, you're quite right," I answered meekly, much to his surprise and to mine.

When I went outside after breakfast, I discovered that Harry *was* quite right. The sun was glorious, and the air was warm but not hot—it still held the heavy, damp coolness of the early morning. How very different it was from the stale, heated air of the sickroom! I breathed it in deeply, smelling the rich odors of the nearby forest and the loamy earth. That was one of the things I enjoyed about my passion for archaeology—the rich smells of the past as we turned over layer after layer of fertile English soil.

Harry had had my horse brought over from the Dower House, and she greeted me as a long-lost friend. She was as glad for the exercise as I, and we raced Harry and his big gray across the fields, almost beating him when we jumped the hedge and made for the woods. The gray's long strides were too much for my Anabel, though, and Harry pulled up ahead of us at the very edge of the forest.

"Almost," I said, laughing, as I reined in Anabel beside his gray. "The next time, we'll gallop down by the spinney, where those turns will try that horse of yours. A guinea says Anabel will outrun you."

"Done! Tomorrow morning?" He paused, his arms folded across his saddle. "Do you realize, Frankie, that this is the very first time I've heard you laugh since I've been here?"

I felt the smile fade from my lips. "I shouldn't be laughing and enjoying myself now. Not with Wykeham struggling for every breath."

"Nonsense." Harry was quite brisk. He smiled, dismounted, and reached up for me. "You need this time away from the sickroom today, just as you're going to need to be out with me tomorrow morning. You'll waste away yourself if you stay indoors all the time.''

He helped me down, his hands firm around my waist as he set me on the ground. I don't know the reason—the morning air, the freedom of the gallop after my imprisonment in the sickroom, the feel of Harry's hands on my waist, or the whimsical half smile on his face as he looked at me—but my knees turned to water, and it was as if there were an iron band around my chest. Harry sensed my mood but said nothing—he simply bent his head and kissed me.

My arms went around his neck and he held me close. It was by no means my first kiss—not even my first kiss from Harry—but it was the first time I had ever experienced such strange emotions. It was as if I were floating—I felt light and warm and comforted, all at once. It was the kind of kiss I had dreamed of when I was younger, and the kind I didn't realize I had missed. I moved closer to him, wanting him to kiss me more, wanting to almost be a part of him. I heard myself say his name as his lips moved to the corners of my mouth. Harry must have sensed my feelings, as he stopped kissing me and held me very close to him. His breathing in my ear was ragged and harsh.

''Marry me, Frankie,'' he whispered.

I stepped back. I wanted to say yes. I wanted to know that I would be kissed like that forever and ever, but I couldn't. Visions of my Roman mosaics floated through my mind. Harry would laugh if I told him of my passion for archaeology, and dismiss it out of hand as the idiosyncrasy of a reclusive female. Of that I was sure. I wanted Harry—of that I was sure, as well—but I also wanted to unearth my mosaics. And there was Wykeham. The thought brought me down to earth with a thud.

''Please, Harry,'' I stammered, for want of anything better to say at the moment. I had to get my thoughts together. All I could think of now was the warm feeling Harry's kiss had left in the pit of my stomach, and the shameful knowledge that I wanted more. I stepped back a step and tried to think about my mosaics and Wykeham.

He chuckled. "Please, what?" He stepped up close to me and put his hands on my shoulders. "Please, another?"

"Yes. No." I caught myself. I was stammering and blushing like some girl just out of the schoolroom. I put my hands on his chest to hold him away from me. "I need a moment, Harry. Please."

He looked at me a moment, then took my hand and put my arm through his. "Let's walk down here, then. David tells me there's a path here between Foxcroft and Pitchley that you and he made when you were small."

I was grateful for his tact and understanding, and gave him a glance of gratitude. I was only now getting my thoughts together and my breathing back to normal. "Yes. I was always over at Pitchley or he was always over here—at least, until he went away to school."

"And you went to London?"

I shook my head. "No, David left early for school. I wanted to go to school, as well, but Papa wouldn't hear of it. He turned me loose in the library at Foxcroft and told me to educate myself."

"Which you did." There was an odd note in his voice.

"Yes. I'm sure you remember how Papa was always busy with Foxcroft or in London, and my stepmothers were either breeding or in the nursery, so I was left quite alone to read and study. I enjoyed my life very much."

He turned and touched my cheek, a smile on his face. "And to think I am attracted to such a bluestocking. My father will certainly be amused."

"I wouldn't think your father could find anything amusing," I replied before I thought. "Especially a bluestocking."

Harry wasn't at all angry, as I had thought he might be. Instead, he laughed as we turned back toward the horses. "Probably not. He would most likely look at me in that stiff way he has and tell me that a bluestocking would be the making of me." He stopped and looked at me until I felt my breathing go ragged again. "Actually he would be delighted to have you in the family, bluestocking or not. You know that both he and your father always hoped we would wed. I'm sure having you as my bride would do more to restore me to his good graces than anything else I could ever do."

He suddenly realized what he had said. "Not that I'm asking you to marry me because of him," he added hastily. "You know how I feel about you—how I've always felt."

"I thought perhaps you and your father had reconciled," I said, ignoring his faux pas and trying to be as tactful as possible.

"We'll never reconcile," he said bitterly. "I've come home, and we tolerate each other since he's the almighty earl and controls the lands and the purse strings. And, by God, don't think he ever lets me forget it."

There was really nothing I could say. "I'm sorry, Harry." It sounded as ineffective as it was.

When he returned to the horses, Harry suddenly said, "Frankie, when I want something, I go after it, and I don't stop until I get it."

"That sounds much more like a threat, Harry, than a declaration." I tried to keep my voice light.

"It's not really a threat, Frankie—it's more of a statement. I want you, and I have since I first saw you all those years ago." He gave me a leg up, then looked at me. "And I mean to have you."

I didn't answer Harry and we didn't discuss the subject further as we rode back toward Foxcroft. Harry meant to marry me, of that I had no doubt, and right now the idea of being near Harry always had its definite attractions. But did I really want to marry? It meant managing a large household, breeding constantly, and always working to ensure one's husband's place in society. It wasn't that I couldn't do those things, or didn't ever wish to, although breeding certainly held no fascination for me after the experiences I had seen my stepmothers endure, but existing merely to ensure one's husband's acceptance in society seemed such a frivolous goal. After that initial rush of calf love had died when Harry left for Jamaica, I had never even thought about myself being married. I could see that if I accepted Harry's offer the pattern of my life would change radically.

I wanted more than to be the perfect wife. I was quite willing to do all of the expected things, but I also wanted the freedom to pursue my studies and unearth my mosaics. Archaeology was a most regrettable ambition for a female—

no man of my acquaintance, including Harry, would stand for his wife digging in the dirt like a common laborer, even if the results were an addition to art and history. I sighed.

"What is it, my pet?" Harry asked, the old familiar smile on his face. "Planning your wedding dress?"

"Hardly." My voice was dry. "Don't count your chickens before they hatch, Harry. I've gotten along fine for five and twenty years without being married, and I imagine I could get along quite well for another five and twenty."

Harry laughed aloud. "Not you, Frankie, not you. Let me tell you something, my girl. You were made to marry and be a wife."

"I don't think so." I heard myself becoming mulish.

"But, yes," he teased. "Since I find you're the betting kind, I'll wager you another guinea that you'll be married within a six-month."

"Done!" There was a note of triumph in my voice, and a great feeling of relief. Now I would have an excuse to put Harry off for at least half a year while I continued my excavations. He had certainly done me a huge favor, albeit unwittingly. I grinned at him. "Now, Harry, it will be useless for you to court me for a six-month because the answer will be no. After all, I have the honor of my family to uphold now."

He laughed and reached for my hand. "Oh, no, Frankie, my girl. Our little wager has only added zest to the game. Now I can begin to court you in earnest. Wait and see." He stopped and looked at me as we came close to the stables. "As a matter of fact, how would you like to increase the wager to, say, a thousand pounds?"

"A guinea will do, Harry. After all, it's merely the principle of the thing, isn't it?"

He laughed again as he helped me dismount. "I see you have all the gaming instincts of a parson. I'm going to have to take you to London and teach you how to gamble." He set me down on the ground, and his touch left me somewhat breathless. "After we're married, of course," he added.

He glanced around to see if we were alone, then kissed me good-bye, quite soundly, before I could answer to this piece of impudence. I was still breathless when I went back into the house to help in the sickroom.

"Well, I see you've finally returned." David's voice was distinctly irritable.

"Harry and I went for a ride. I needed the fresh air." I was feeling wonderful again and certainly didn't intend to put up with David being a gudgeon.

"And I needed someone to help me, Frankie. Come here."

I repressed a desire to point out that Brooks, Perkins, and Mrs. Simms had been there to help. Instead, I looked at David's harried face and walked slowly over to the bed. To my consternation, I saw that Wykeham looked very much worse. I hadn't thought it possible, but he was. He was ghastly white and was thrashing around on the bed. "Is his fever worse?" I whispered to David.

He nodded. "It seemed to come on anew last night. I thought it was beginning to break a little and the worst was over. Now it appears it has just begun again. Would you sponge him with cool water and alcohol for a while?"

David left the room, and I poured lavender water onto a cloth. The beauty of the morning, the ride, my feelings when Harry had kissed me, all were forgotten. Right now, the earl's condition was the only thing that had any reality to it.

The sound of his harsh breathing filled the stuffy room, and every time I looked at his deathly pale face, I keenly felt that his suffering was my fault. Guilt was a fairly new emotion for me, and I found that I didn't care for it.

I wrung out the cloth and sponged his face gently, smoothing his dark hair back from his forehead. There were strands of gray threaded there that marked it. He was burning hot, and he tossed and mumbled in his sleep, almost making an effort to rise. With difficulty, I held him down. If he didn't quiet soon, I was going to have to wake Perkins, who was sleeping in a chair.

At least, I thought to myself grimly as I sponged him over and over and tried to keep him from moving, *I do have the satisfaction of knowing that I've done everything for Wykeham that I can.*

It wasn't very much satisfaction.

Chapter 6

The next several days were a blur. I was afraid to leave the earl. I took double shifts, not out of sympathy, but out of fear that he might die because I hadn't done enough. We carefully administered laudanum drops, tried to spoon barley water and broth past his unwilling lips, and sponged him with lavender water and alcohol. By the third day of this new bout of fever we were exhausted, dirty, and unkempt. I had barely left his bedside since my ride with Harry. The ride and Harry's kiss seemed an age ago—I hadn't even spoken to Harry since, except to exchange hasty words about the earl's chances of living.

Wykeham had been near death and back several times during those days. David had refused to leave the room and had asked old Dr. Larson in the next parish to see to his other patients. He shouted at me when I tried to get him to rest. I was so exhausted that I completely forgot my manners and shouted right back at him. Actually, I felt the better for doing it, but we both stopped guiltily when Wykeham moaned—the noise had aroused him.

I was sitting by the bedside sponging Wykeham on the early afternoon of the third day when I heard him make sounds as if he were trying to speak. I bent my head as he whispered hoarsely.

"What?" I asked him. "What do you want?" I leaned close to his lips to hear him.

David was at my side in an instant. "What did he say?" he asked anxiously. "Is he coherent? Did you understand him? What did he want?"

I felt myself blush furiously. "He seems to be talking about . . . He mentioned . . ." I could go no further.

David shook my shoulders. "What, Frankie?" His voice was harsh.

I fought to keep the blush from my face, but I couldn't look David in the eye. "He seems to be talking about a woman."

"What?" This time, David's voice was incredulous.

"That's what he said. It sounded distinctly as if he said 'Nancy,' and when I asked him to repeat it, he said 'She's a sweet'—there was another word in there that I didn't understand—'my Nancy.' "

"Nancy? A woman?" David acted as if he had never heard the words.

I was becoming somewhat exasperated. "Those were his exact words, David. If you want to know whom he's talking about, I suggest you ask Perkins. I don't know." Doggedly, I kept on sponging. David looked at me and left the room. I supposed he was going to find Perkins, who had finally been persuaded to get some fresh air.

It was a beautiful day outside—the sun was warm and a soft breeze was blowing—but inside, the room was so hot and close that my gown was damp from sweat and my hair hung in tendrils against my face and neck. No wonder Wykeham had a hard time breathing, I thought to myself—the air was so hot and stale that even I had difficulty.

"Nancy," he said again. His voice was a low moan.

I leaned over to him. "Nancy isn't here. Be still." I wiped his face with lavender water and felt his skin. It was so hot the cloth instantly became warm. "No wonder you're burning with fever," I said, as much to myself as to him. "This room would roast a goose." I could stand it no longer—I got up and opened the windows, then threw back all the covers on him except a sheet.

It was almost an hour before David returned. He was horrified to find a soft breeze stirring through the room and the air in it a reasonable temperature at last. "You'll kill him with this air," he yelled at me, scrambling to close the windows.

"But David, I believe his fever has gone down."

David felt his patient's brow and hand, then walked over and reopened the windows, pulling the drapes aside to let in as much fresh air as possible. "At this point, I'll try anything," he said, not looking at me. "God knows it can't hurt him any. Maybe you've hit on something, Frankie." I bit my tongue to keep from saying "I told you so."

"He does seem cooler." David sat and felt his pulse. "I believe the fever is breaking."

"Either that or he's dying," I muttered. I had almost come to believe that he would die simply to spite me. I knew it wasn't logical, but I was too exhausted to think clearly.

David and I were joined shortly by Perkins and, after persuading him that leaving the windows open was the best course, we sat and watched the patient carefully. Charlotte came in, carrying our nuncheon on a tray, as well as some broth for Wykeham. I tried again to spoon some down him, but only succeeded in dampening the sheets.

By late afternoon, the earl's breathing had lost its hoarse edge and he had quieted. David said that was an excellent sign, so I took heart and left for a much-needed nap. I hated to leave, but it was either that or fall into a heap on the floor.

Charlotte woke me at midnight so I could take my shift. She was as frazzled as the rest of us, but she had thought to bring me some chocolate. Charlotte had, I thought, overcome her first impression of me and had become quite attentive. "Have you had word on the earl's condition?" I asked.

"Brooks says as how his lordship is much improved," she said cautiously. To my complete chagrin, word had rapidly gotten out as to the exact nature of the earl's wound and how he had received it. Harry had informed me that he had heard it from the vicar's daughter. I didn't think to ask him what he had been doing talking with the vicar's daughter, a poor girl who has had her cap set for a rich husband far longer than is seemly. She had spots and a milk-toast disposition—definitely not a woman who could ever manage Harry.

As for the news of the earl's injury, which seemed to be spreading and would, without a doubt, eventually reach as far as London and every gossip in the *ton*, I secretly blamed

Griggins, but had no proof of it. At any rate, the household staff, as well as the inhabitants of the Dower House, seemed to think I was one step from the gallows. Actually, there had been moments when I had thought so, as well.

Charlotte bustled around my chamber, readying my hairbrushes. She was fast becoming a wizard with a brush and comb. "I think his lordship is some better," she ventured, without looking at me. "Leastways, that's what Griggins told me."

"Is his fever still down?"

Charlotte jerked at my unruly hair and nodded her head vigorously. "Perkins came down for supper with us, and he allowed as that the earl was on the mend."

"Really? Perkins said that?" This was indeed news. If Perkins was persuaded the earl was improving, then it must be so. "I'm delighted to hear that, Charlotte."

"Yes, milady." She paused, shoving parts of my hair here and there, then sighed, contentedly. "Would you like a bath?"

I looked down at my rumpled gown. It did look the worse for wear. "I don't have time for a bath, Charlotte, but I will change."

Charlotte was overjoyed. "This, milady, you must wear this." She brought out a sprigged muslin that Katie had packed. It was not at all suitable for nursing.

"The other brown gown will do, Charlotte."

From her expression of dismay, I could see that I had offended her, but it could not be helped. "Perhaps tomorrow."

Her smile returned as she laid out the brown gown. "Very good, milady."

To my surprise, Wykeham was sleeping quietly and his breathing sounded almost regular. I glanced at David and Perkins. They were smiling broadly.

"The fever's broken," David said. "He's going to be just fine—barring pneumonia, of course," he added.

"Of course," I replied. Did the man have no optimism at all?

Without difficulty, I persuaded Perkins and David to retire for the night. They were both completely exhausted, and they left with only token resistance. I assured them I would call them immediately if there was any change in the earl's condition.

After they left, I sat in the large, upholstered chair by the bed. I placed a small branch of candles on the table, and pulled a rug over my knees. I took a good, long look at Wykeham. He was breathing regularly and deeply. He had lost weight—the bones in his face were prominent now— and there was a bluish tinge under his eyes, but I was struck by the fact that, thin and pale as he was, he was still singularly handsome. He was not anywhere as handsome as Harry, but he looked as if he were a strong man—one the tenants and villagers could rely on to watch out for their interests and be fair with them. Responsible and dependable, as my father would have said. They were very good traits for an earl, I thought to myself, remembering that Papa had been much the same way. Maybe, if Papa had known him, he would have been reconciled to having the damned rebel whelp as the earl at Foxcroft. I smiled to myself at the thought.

I forced my eyes to open wide. I would have to be vigilant during the night or I would doze. I was nodding when I heard the clock chime the hour and resolutely sat up at attention. I've never been one to shirk my duty.

"Do you know that you snore?"

I jerked awake with a start. "What?" I asked in confusion. Then, to my complete horror, I discovered that it was daylight. I had slept through the night. I looked around to see who was speaking.

"Do you know you snore?" The voice was low and weak, but held a distinct note of laughter. I looked around again and discovered Wykeham's eyes upon me. I forgot my manners and stared. He had, without a doubt, eyes of the deepest turquoise that I had ever seen. I felt almost giddy just looking at them.

"I most certainly do not! Ladies do not snore." I tore my eyes from his and managed to stammer a reply.

"Oh, yes," he answered, with a feeble attempt at a smile. "A perfectly ladylike snore, but a snore nevertheless." His voice was wavering.

I tried to get up from my chair, but my foot had gone to

sleep and I was tangled in the rug. For a moment I wobbled there, tottering over him. It was touch and go as to whether I fell on the earl or back into the chair. With a great effort, I managed to sprawl backwards into the chair.

"Thank you," he mumbled, favoring me with a charming smile. Then he closed his eyes and either slept or slipped into unconsciousness again. I reached over and felt his forehead. He was only a little warm.

I had to wait until feeling returned to my foot before I could get up and hobble down the corridor to rouse David. In my eagerness to spread the good news, it didn't occur to me that I had left Wykeham unattended.

"How could you?" David ranted at me. I had thought he would be overjoyed that the earl had awakened and was lucid and evidently on the mend. Indeed, he almost ran over me in his rush to the bedside, but more, I think, because he believed the man was going to do himself some harm right there in the bed, than to see a miracle.

"Did you say he spoke to you?" David finally said to me after examining his now sleeping patient. It took that to convince him that Wykeham was all of one piece.

"Yes, he spoke, and even tried to smile."

"Wonderful. What did he say? Did he describe his condition?"

I paused. I certainly didn't wish to divulge that the man had informed me that I snored. "No, he didn't describe his condition." It wasn't a lie at all.

"Well, what did he say, then, Frankie? You did understand him, didn't you?"

"Perfectly well, David. And what he had to say had no bearing on his illness, let me assure you."

David looked sharply at me and then smiled. "Ah, Nancy again."

It took me a moment to recall who Nancy was, but I decided that was an excellent out. Since I didn't wish to lie, I merely smiled charmingly at David. He, in turn, gave me a conspiratorial wink.

Perkins came running in, received the good news, and had to be restrained from awakening his master on the spot. As it was, he sat by the bedside while David suggested I go on to bed. "You need your rest, Frankie," David said with concern.

"I'm fine," I answered, trying not to mention that I had been dozing for the entire night. Not snoring, however.

Right there, in front of Perkins, David gave me a big hug, much to my surprise. I hadn't seen him in such high spirits since we were children. "No, Frankie, my little helper, I want you to get some rest."

I was wide awake and had no intention of going to bed again. "I'll just stay up a while, David—I'm too excited by the earl's recovery to sleep. Perhaps you should go rest."

He shook his head. "No, I'm going on down to breakfast."

Breakfast! The very word made my mouth water. I was practically starving, and certainly not sleepy after spending the night dozing in the chair, so I nobly offered to breakfast with David. He seemed to think it was a touch of martyrdom on my part, which I didn't like, but didn't know how to correct. Oh, what a tangled web we weave, and so on.

"When will the earl be up and around so we can all go home?" I asked between bites of muffin.

"Oh, it will be weeks yet."

I choked and started coughing. "Weeks!" I finally gasped, my eyes watering. "I can't stay here for weeks!" I coughed again and felt my face turn red. "Can't you do something?"

"Here, drink some tea." David pressed a fresh cup on me. "Are you all right? As for doing something, there's not much I can do for your cough until that bite of muffin goes down."

"You misunderstand me," I said, draining an entire cup of tea and scalding my tongue in the process. "Now, I'm perfectly fine," I said, catching my breath and pouring my teacup full of milk to cool my tongue. Evidently, David wasn't going to answer me until my health had returned. I took a deep breath. "What I was asking was if you could do something about finding a nurse for the earl. Or do you really think it will be weeks before I can return home?"

"Return home?" He seemed puzzled. "Oh, I see what you're saying. No, you can return home as soon as you care to—tomorrow or the next day. It will be weeks, however, before Wykeham will be strong enough to be out and around.''

His words were like music to my ears. Visions of my mosaics floated in front of my eyes and I felt a blissful smile cross my face. At last!

''Oh, I see.'' David smiled indulgently at me. ''I never thought to see you head over heels, Frankie.'' He sighed. ''I suppose that means the rest of us are out of the running.''

''What?'' I stared at him. David, along with the rest of the village, knew of my passion for digging in the dirt. ''Head over heels? That's a strange way to put things but, yes, I suppose you could say that.'' I laughed.

''Harry's quite a catch, from what I hear. I wish you well.''

''Harry?'' I was past puzzled. ''David, will you please stop talking in riddles. Whatever are you saying?''

He laughed. ''I saw that smile on your face, Frankie. You're in love if I ever saw it, and I can only presume the lucky man is Harry. After all, he's been a regular visitor here, and it certainly isn't because he has an acquaintance with Wykeham.'' He paused and looked impishly at me. ''Besides, I do recall that once you did have your cap set for him.''

''Of all the things to say to me, David! Love, indeed! And furthermore, I have *never* had my cap set for anyone. I thought you were my friend.'' I was righteously indignant.

His booming laugh filled the breakfast room. ''Oh, but I am your friend, Frankie. And as a doctor, I'd say you had a bad case of lovesickness. I remember well, back when you were around sixteen—I was one and twenty then—you were in alt over Harry, and I was crestfallen because I had returned from Edinburgh and you hadn't even noticed I was alive.''

''You? I've always noticed you, David.'' I missed his point.

He shook his head. ''Not the way you noticed Harry,'' he said with a wry smile.

''Harry is simply my friend,'' I said haughtily, feeling a touch of a telltale blush creep up my face. ''If you must know, I was not thinking of Harry at all. I was smiling because I was thinking of my digs."

"Really?" David was unable to disguise his skepticism.

"Really. You should know me well enough by now to know what's important in my life, David."

"Uuumm." He didn't look convinced. "Is your latest project coming on that well?" David leaned back in his chair and looked at me. "I remember that you once talked me into digging into a mound by the stables. You were convinced that a Roman general was buried there because it was so large."

"I was quite young then, David, and not so well versed in my history."

He grinned at me. "Yes, your father was upset to find us digging up the remains of a horse. As I recall, he felt it improper behavior for a young lady of twelve."

"As I recall, you felt the same." My voice was dry.

He had the courtesy to look chagrined. "Yes, but you managed to override all my objections, as usual. I hope Harry's a stronger man than I am, or you'll have him broken in no time at all."

I felt my mouth fall open as I searched for a suitable reply. As I could think of no rejoinder, I contented myself with glaring at him. "There are times when you push friendship too far, David," I finally managed to say.

He laughed heartily. "One thing I know, Frankie—no matter which lucky man finally wins you, his life will never have a dull moment." He rose and left, still laughing.

I sat a few minutes, trying to sort out if I had just been insulted or complimented. With David, one never knew. I smiled to myself as I thought of him. Since I could remember, David and I had played together, and I suppose he was my dearest friend in all the world. If I ever needed anything, I knew I could turn to him and he would help me, no questions asked. And I would do the same for him.

Standing, I noted there was no one around, and took the moment to yawn luxuriously. The whole day stretched out in front of me and, at last, there wasn't the constant anxiety of Wykeham's flirt with death to occupy every waking moment. I hadn't realized how much I had worried about the man. Right now, knowing he would most likely recover quite nicely, I felt as though a huge weight had been lifted from my shoulders. I thought wryly that his recovery was almost better for me than for him.

Outside, it was a glorious day. The sun was shining, there was a little breeze, and all was right with the world. I would go home for the morning, check on my sisters, and take a quick turn around my digs. I couldn't wait to cut some cross trenches and explore further. Then let David make jokes about my latest project.

For the first time in ages I had something to look forward to. I almost bounded up the stairs.

─────────── **Chapter 7** ───────────

Charlotte was lurking in the hall when I went upstairs, and in just a moment she had the tub brought in, and two burly footmen followed carrying cans of hot water. I complimented her on her foresight.

Sinking into the tub was heavenly, and I soaked until the water began to get cold. Then Charlotte took me in hand and brushed my hair until I thought it was going to come out. After I decided I was going to survive that, I had to admit that the results were quite good. I had meant to put on another plain gown, but Charlotte carefully got out the sprigged muslin, and to avoid a disagreement, I put it on. "There," she said, putting the final touches on my hair, "you look quite the thing."

Looking at myself in the mirror, I had to agree. "You're marvelous, Charlotte," I said warmly, and was rewarded by a flood of tears and an "Oh, Lady Frances!" as she ran out of the room. I stared after her in amazement: did nothing work with Charlotte? Perhaps when I went back to the Dower House, the poor girl's life would return to normal.

As I quickly went across the small path toward the Dower

House, I was aware of everything—the scent of the grass, the colors of the flowers, the sounds of the birds. I felt free for the first time in a long while. It rather surprised me—I had felt weighted down with responsibility, but I hadn't realized that my sense of obligation toward Wykeham had been so strong.

All, as I had expected, was utter chaos at the Dower House. The furniture looked as if it hadn't been dusted since I was last there, and there was distinct evidence that things had been hastily picked up and stashed away when the servants had seen me coming. And the girls! I was really going to have to replace Mademoiselle DeSalle without delay. Babs had put her hair up. I made her take it down immediately, which threw her into a fit of the sulks. She stalked off to her room, threatening to run away to London and people who appreciated her. Annie was much the same, not paying attention to anything or anyone around her, while Charlie was a disaster. She was covered with layers of dog fur and mud. The child couldn't have been washed in days. I suspected that she had even been sleeping in her clothing. When I questioned her, I discovered that things were even worse than I had imagined—not only had she been sleeping in her clothing, but the dog had been sleeping in the bed with her. I immediately set the maids to scrubbing down both Charlie and her room, as well as giving her bed a scouring. I threatened to banish the dog to the stables, but gave in to Charlie's wailing. I did forbid her to sleep with the creature.

The household somewhat in hand, I decided I indeed did have the time to walk up to my digs before going back to Foxcroft.

I had almost reached the field when there was a yell behind me. "Frankie, wait up!" I turned to find Harry coming toward me at a canter. He had a marvelous seat and even I had to admit that he looked dashing and handsome sitting atop the gray. He had on a coat of blue superfine that was cut superbly, and his breeches were so snug as to appear painted on. When he pulled up beside me and my eyes were on a level with those legs, I felt a small shiver go down my spine. Harry was quite a man.

"And what's a beautiful lady like you doing walking the fields this morning?" he asked with a charming smile, effortlessly dismounting to walk beside me.

Unaccountably, I felt a small twinge of dismay that Harry should be here to spoil my pleasure in looking at my digs. I knew he wouldn't understand, and however was I going to explain my work to him? Even worse, I was surprised to discover that I was somewhat ashamed of what I did, as though digging in the fields to discover artifacts was not at all proper. To my chagrin, I realized that Harry would *not* think it proper.

I lifted my chin. "Checking on my digs," I said defiantly.

"Your what?" He was puzzled.

We had reached the edge of the field, and I glanced up toward my mounds of dirt before I answered him. Instead of explaining, I froze in complete shock. For the first time in my life, I screeched.

"What is it, Frankie? What do you see?"

"How could he?" I sputtered, staring at a freshly ploughed, leveled field. "How *could* he?"

"How could who do what?" Harry was fast becoming exasperated.

"Pembroke! It had to be Pembroke!" I screamed. "Wait until I get my hands on him!" I left Harry standing in amazement and started running across the newly ploughed field, with no thought for the destruction of my slippers. The ground had been freshly ploughed and leveled, the rich earth turned up not long before. I guessed it had been done only three or four days ago.

I hopped from furrow to furrow, clutching my sprigged muslin halfway up to my knees with no thought for propriety. Finally, I reached the approximate place where my trenches had been located. Cold fury gripped me. There was absolutely no trace of my hard work. To my surprise, I stood in the middle of the field and began to cry.

Harry caught up with me and put his hands on my shoulders. "Frankie, for God's sake, tell me what's wrong. Sweetheart, why are you crying?"

"All my work," I sobbed, putting my head on his shoulder and bawling right into Harry's blue superfine. He stood mute and patted me on the back while I blubbered like a baby. Finally, the tears stopped. I broke loose from him and bent down to scratch through the dirt with my hands.

"Good God, Frankie, whatever are you doing?" Harry was scandalized to see me groveling in the dirt.

"It's all gone," I wailed. "There's nothing left of all that work. It's all his fault." I was ready to start blubbering again. There was no trace at all of my careful trenches. It would all have to be done over. I stood and mopped at my face with my fingers.

"Now you've done it," Harry said with a grin as he produced a handkerchief. "You've streaked your whole face with dirt. You, my dear Frankie, look a perfect ragamuffin." He dabbed at my face with the clean white linen.

"Thank you," I managed to say through sniffs. "I'm glad you brought a handkerchief."

"Gentlemen are always prepared to rescue a damsel in distress," he said, still dabbing. I took the handkerchief from him and scrubbed at my face vigorously.

"Is that better?"

He stood back and looked critically at me. "Yes, but now, my dear, you look as red as a lobster." He took my elbow. "I must admit I'm a little confused, Frankie. Why don't we leave the middle of this field, and you can tell me what the fuss is all about."

I took a last look around, angry now. "It's going to be more than a fuss, Harry. I can promise Pembroke that much."

I stalked across the dirt, sinking into the loam with every step. There was dirt on my hands, dirt on my petticoat, dirt on my gown, and dirt in my slippers. I didn't care. Harry gave up trying to save the gloss on his Hessians and caught up with me. By this time, I had reached the path. "Frankie, for heaven's sake, will you please explain yourself?"

"It should be perfectly plain, Harry."

He rolled his eyes heavenward. "Oh, of course. I find you merrily walking along the path this morning, apparently enjoying the weather, then you come to the field. All at once you begin screaming like a banshee, dash out across the furrows, and start crying. Yes, it's all perfectly plain."

I paused while Harry untied his horse and we began walking. "I'm sorry, Harry. Perhaps I should explain that I had spent a great deal of time digging in this field, and Pembroke has seen fit to plough up my work. I shall have to begin again."

He looked puzzled, then brightened. "Digging? Oh, you've been gardening! My dear, why didn't you tell me? I think every woman should have something to keep her occupied. My mother, rest her soul, was very fond of roses."

"Harry, I'm afraid you don't understand . . ." I began.

"Oh, of course I do, Frankie, and I think gardening is a wonderful little hobby for you. After all, a woman needs something besides her husband and children to fill up her life. I do think you should consider planting your flowers closer to the house, though. Out in the fields here doesn't seem quite the proper place."

I was quite speechless, but that didn't deter Harry. "Perhaps you can visit my Aunt Ella and let her show you how to grow roses," he offered. "It would give the two of you something to talk about."

There was nothing for it except to take the plunge before he had me refurbishing the royal conservatory. "Harry, I abhor gardening," I said flatly. "What I've been doing is much more important. I've been searching for Roman ruins."

He laughed heartily. "Frankie, what a quiz you are," he said when he caught his breath. "That's ridiculous."

"Ridiculous or not, it's what I've been doing. I'm an avid antiquarian."

Harry stopped and looked at me, puzzled. "Well, my dear, why don't you just go to a museum and look at those things all cleaned up? There's no use in you dashing around and getting in the dirt."

"Harry," I said in a most reasonable tone, "I'm very much interested in archaeology. I *like* digging in the dirt. That's what archaeology is all about—digging for artifacts."

Harry stared at me for a full minute, then began laughing again. "Trust you to try to shock me, Frankie, and, I do admit, you almost did for a moment. My dear girl, if you need something to take up your time, I'm sure that you'll have your hands full with the household and the nursery when we're married." He smiled sunnily at me while I stared at him, openmouthed. "Now, come along," he said, as though he were talking to a spaniel, "we need to get you cleaned up. You've got dirt all over you."

"Harry," I began, but he interrupted me, patting me on the hand. "Now, hush, dear. I understand completely, and I'm sure you'll soon put this foolishness behind you. Come along." He started toward the Dower House, and I walked along beside him, biting my tongue to keep from screaming at him.

Harry left me at the Dower House and returned to Pitchley. I went up to change and reflect on what had happened. I swore that Pembroke would get his comeuppance, one way or another. Harry was another matter. I had known what his reaction would be, but that didn't make it any easier to take. I tossed my sprigged muslin down on the floor in disgust. *Men*, I thought. They always thought they were so superior. And the worst part was that I could do very little about it.

On the day after my discovery of Pembroke's outrage, I received a hastily scribbled note from Harry saying that his father had recalled him to London. It seemed that he had business in Brussels and wanted his son to go along. Harry had to leave immediately and didn't sound at all enthusiastic. He did include several protestations of love and affection, as well as a comment on our marriage. I fervently prayed that he had better sense than to spread such a false rumor all over London. I also realized guiltily that I was somewhat glad to have him gone for a week or two—I needed the time to gather my wits and think. For some reason, when Harry was around, I didn't seem to be able to think clearly. He had a very strange effect on me, which I found most disturbing.

From that day, I stayed at the Dower House and went over to Foxcroft every day to see Wykeham. He was definitely on the mend, but not yet strong. I sat with him, most of the time watching him sleep, but occasionally talking with him. He was very interested in Foxcroft and the title—evidently, his father hadn't spoken very much about it. I was able to fill him in on the history of the house and family, and even went down to the library and got some genealogical records to read to him. I also asked about his family, hoping to find out about the woman he had mentioned, but although he mentioned several brothers and sisters, there was no Nancy. I did ask if he was married, and he laughed and told me no. At that point, I decided Nancy was the soon-to-be Lady Wykeham.

I had been quite embarrassed at first, wondering how he would feel when he discovered that I had shot him. I was trying to get up the courage to tell him when he mentioned it. It seemed David had beaten me to it.

"I hear you're a crack shot," Wykeham had said as I sat beside him, pausing in my reading of Miss Austen's novel.

My face turned bright red as I tried to regain my composure. "Most of the time," I managed to say.

He chuckled. "I didn't mean to embarrass you. Watterson tells me that you were responsible for this, but you were also responsible for saving my life. Thank you."

"I thought you were a poacher," I blurted out. "I didn't mean to hurt you—only to wing you so you could be brought to trial. You moved unexpectedly." The words came out in a rush. "I'm not making any excuses," I said, catching myself. "I only wanted to explain."

"No explanation necessary," he said. "It's over and done with, and I'm on the mend now. We don't have to mention it again." He smiled at me, and his turquoise eyes were friendly.

"Thank you," I said.

"Now, back to Miss Austen," he said. "I don't mean to insult your taste in reading material, but could you possibly find something else? Miss Austen is a very fine writer, but not at all to my taste. Perhaps the infamous Lord Byron, or would that offend you?"

"Not at all," I said with relief. "Lord Byron it is."

Wykeham asked me to call him by his given name—Jefferson—but I couldn't. I had called him Wykeham so often that the name was second nature to me. He was on the mend now, and as soon as he was able, he had Perkins carry him down to the library, and we began to meet there daily. He seemed glad for me to show him the records and point out information about the estate.

I had been waiting for the right moment to complain about Pembroke, and it came one rainy day as we were sitting in the library playing chess, one of Wykeham's favorite pastimes. There was a fire blazing to keep off the damp chill, and the place was altogether cozy. I waited until Wykeham was quite relaxed before I brought it up. I thought about letting him win just to get him in a better mood, but discarded the thought as dishonest.

I pondered a move and gauged his mood as he sat sipping tea across from me. "There." I looked over at him. "Your move." While he looked at the board, I brought up my topic casually. "Have you met Mr. Pembroke yet?"

He looked at me over the rim of his teacup and grinned. "I wondered when you'd bring that up."

"I'm sure I don't know what you mean."

He laughed. "Pembroke told me you'd be over here in a flaming rage, and I waited for days for you to come screaming to the house."

"The nerve of the man! I'd certainly never come screaming into anyone's house, much less this one." I gave him a withering glance as he chuckled. "I merely wished to ask if you had met the man and were aware of his plans."

"Oh, yes, he's told me all about his plans. Evidently, a large part of his plan is to thwart your plans. From what I gathered, you and Pembroke have been at loggerheads for a long while. I must confess I was somewhat confused about what's going on." He put his teacup down and moved a chess piece. "Perhaps you could tell me."

I hesitated to, but there was no other way. "Unlike your country, England is rich with history," I began.

He nodded, but interrupted me gently. "America is quite rich in history, as well, but aside from that, I suppose England could be called my country now."

"True," I said. I hadn't thought of that at all. He seemed somewhat a foreigner—everything bespoke it, from his slightly drawling accent to his choice of words to his amazingly liberal outlook on life.

"You were telling me about the contretemps between you and Pembroke," he said, leaning back in his chair and sipping his tea without much relish. The chessboard was temporarily forgotten.

I decided to be as frank with him as I had been with Harry and get his reaction over and done with. "I'm an antiquarian," I said, somewhat belligerently.

"I noticed your enthusiasm for history," he said, sipping more tea. "I've always enjoyed history, but sadly never got to study it at length." He paused, looking at me, a slight frown on his thin face. "Exactly what does an antiquarian do?"

"Perhaps you prefer the term *archaeologist*," I said. "I'm trying to find the remains of a Roman villa here." I sat still and waited for his laugh.

Instead, he poured himself more tea and filled my cup, as well. "Interesting. Have you had any success?"

I stared at him. I was completely unprepared for this reaction, and I wondered briefly if he was having fun at my expense. But, he was looking steadily at me with those turquoise eyes and he was perfectly serious. "Yes," I stammered, "I have. I've found some bits of bronze, and before Pembroke ploughed the field over, I had unearthed some tiles from a mosaic. I think they might be part of a larger floor, perhaps the main room of a villa. There were several villas recorded in this area."

"Finding a villa is important to you, isn't it?"

I nodded. I had never been able to discuss my avocation with anyone without facing ridicule. Even David thought it was humorous, so Wykeham's reaction left me almost speechless.

There was a silence as Wykeham sipped tea. It was a comfortable silence, and I began to relax. He smiled at me again and put his teacup down. "I knew you'd be doing something useful," he said, looking once again at the chessboard. "Your move."

"But, what about Pembroke?" I blurted out, reaching for a piece and moving it.

Wykeham glanced at me. "I'll speak to him about leaving your field alone. I imagine there are other fields he can use for planting his turnips."

"Oh, thank you!" I was ecstatic.

"You're welcome," he said, reaching across the board to make his move.

Wykeham insisted I take his carriage back to the Dower House so I wouldn't get wet or chilled. When I got there, I prepared to make the mad dash from the carriage to the house (we were not blessed with a porte cochere), but there were two carriages in the driveway blocking my way. It took me a moment to recognize the crest. Evidently, Lizzie had arrived from London and was probably in the house wreaking havoc. She always did that. I never saw how poor Bassworth stood it, but he seemed besotted with her. She probably kept him in such a state of confusion that he couldn't think. But then, Bassworth wasn't noted for thinking very much anyway. He was perfectly suited for Lizzie, I thought.

When I got inside, Jervis frowned at the puddles I dripped onto the floor, but I ignored him. "Is Lizzie here?" I asked.

He nodded a fraction of an inch. "Lady Bassworth has arrived," he said in his stiffest voice.

"Good," I said, heading for the stairs, leaving a soggy trail behind me. Jervis called for a maid.

Upstairs was an uproar. I could hear Babs chattering, Lizzie babbling, and Charlie's puppy yelping. I decided to forgo the pleasures of family until I had changed. After that, I would have to brave them.

All too soon I had to go to Lizzie's old room, where everyone was gathered. Lizzie rushed to greet me, and enveloped me in a great cloud of powder and perfume as she embraced me. She was quite overdressed—all the crack of fashion, I assumed. "Well, Lizzie, you're looking quite fetching," I said when I had managed to extricate myself from her hold. "Very much the London lady."

"Do you think so?" Lizzie asked, pirouetting so I could see her dress, which was altogether cut too low and was of a rather bad shade of yellow. I thought Lizzie looked rather jaundiced in it, but I wasn't one to say so.

"It's certainly fashionable," I commented.

"I love it," Babs gushed. "Lizzie has promised it to me when she's tired of it. I can't wait."

"I'm not sure that's your color," I said to Babs, but she paid no attention. She was full of her news.

"Oh, Frankie, Lizzie's promised to take me to London with her for a few weeks. Say I can go, please. I want to. Lizzie says it will be good for me to see the town before I go to be presented. After all I need to *see* these famous things, and perhaps get a glimpse of the people I'll meet once I've come out." She thankfully ran out of breath and had to stop for a second. Out of long practice, I smoothly cut in. "No," I said. "You're much too young to be carousing around London, and Lizzie hasn't time to watch you."

Babs set up a wail that sounded like a dying hound, and I was forced to banish her to her room for a few minutes so the rest of us could talk. It was only then that I saw the poor woman cringing against the wall, staring at the lot of us like a scared rabbit. After the first look, I knew who she was. She had much the same look as Babs—the pale skin, blue eyes, and wild, frizzy red hair. She had tried to tame her hair, but it stood out in wisps all over her head, with part of it shoved into an untidy bun at the back of her head.

"You must be Clara Conroy," I said. I suddenly recalled my letter. The poor woman was unable to do anything except nod. "We're delighted to have you, of course," I said. She nodded again.

I tried again. "As you see, the girls certainly need someone with a firm hand. I hope you'll be able to bring them into line."

She nodded again, and looked from one of us to the other. She was clutching a book that looked suspiciously like one of the Minerva Press romance novels. I had misgivings about that. Her gaze finally settled on Charlie's puppy. The puppy, sensing a kindred spirit, bounded up on her lap and began licking her face. Clara didn't move.

I removed the puppy and gave it to Charlie with instructions to take it outside. Charlie set up a wail that matched Babs's, and finally Clara spoke. "I love puppies," she said, reaching for it and settling it back on her lap, right on top of her marbleized book cover. Charlie promptly sat down at

Clara's feet and looked at me triumphantly. I knew when I was beaten, and turned to Lizzie.

"Surely, you can't be serious about taking Babs to London," I said. "Do you know what you're getting into?"

"Certainly, I do," Lizzie said, acting every inch the grand lady with me. "Bassworth and I would love to have her for company, and it would do her good to get a little town bronze. You don't know the agonies I went through learning what's proper with the *ton*."

"Bosh," I said. "You'd been to London enough to know what to do and what not to do."

She looked at me, victorious. "There. *I* had been to London and so had you, but poor Babs has seldom been. She was still in the nursery and didn't get to go with us. She needs the experience."

"It's her experience I'm worried about," I told Lizzie. "You don't know what Babs is like lately."

"She's just a child," Lizzie said.

"Little do you know, Lizzie." I made a face at her. "I will, however, think about it. Much as I hate to admit it, she might do well in London, but only with the proper supervision."

Lizzie was indignant. "Are you implying that I can't give my own sister the proper supervision?"

"Oh, no," I said hastily. "I'm merely saying that you'd need to be on your toes."

"I'll manage just fine," Lizzie said haughtily. "After all, I'm a married woman now."

I didn't think that fact signified, but I let it pass.

Chapter 8

Lizzie stayed for upwards of a week, creating total chaos. It rained the whole week and we were forced to stay indoors, which made things even worse, if possible. I looked forward to my daily visits to Foxcroft as an oasis of peace and quiet. Wykeham had been in the library every day, and we played chess, read to each other, or just talked. It was the only thing that kept me sane that week.

Wykeham was doing wonderfully—walking a little around the house and grounds, and learning about the estate. He still tired very easily, however, and both Perkins and I were on the watch for this. Our biggest problem was that Wykeham refused to acknowledge it when he was in pain or tired. This day he had looked somewhat drawn, and Perkins, who had decided I was to be trusted, had confided to me that Wykeham was in pain. We decided it was caused by the rainy weather and made plans to keep him occupied indoors. I tried letting him beat me at chess, but got wrapped up in the game, and soon it was a real match. Wykeham and I were almost evenly matched as chess players.

I had been particularly curious about why he had decided to leave America and come back to Foxcroft. I had wondered for several days how to bring the subject up, and, as usual, decided the best way was to approach it obliquely. We were playing chess again in the library, and Perkins had seen that there was a roaring fire built there. Mrs. Simms had brought in some hot spiced wine. We were so hot in the room that we waited until we were alone, then opened the windows, poured out our wine, and sat down to resume our game. "By the way," I mentioned casually, "just why did you decide to leave America and come to Foxcroft?"

He glanced at me in surprise and then laughed aloud. "I wondered when that one was coming," he said. "Actually, I thought you'd probably insinuate it into the conversation somewhere."

"I thought that's what I did," I told him. "The picture of grace and tact. I've always been thought of in that way."

"But, of course." He stood and removed his coat, draping it over the back of the chair. "I hope I don't have to stand on ceremony with you, but it's blasted hot in here, even with the windows open."

"Fine. Save ceremony for when you have to face the *ton*," I said, then waited until he sat back down.

"I don't care to face the *ton*," he said. "I'm also not sure about making a speech in the House of Lords. I'd probably scandalize everyone there with my radical American views."

"Perhaps," I said. "Speaking of America—"

"Like a dog with a bone, aren't you?" he said with a laugh. "I was getting to my story."

"But taking your time about it," I pointed out.

He rang for coffee and leaned back in his chair. "To tell the truth, I really don't know why I came here. I had no interest in leaving Virginia, and as for land, I had more there than is here."

"Are you homesick?" I asked, amazed. That possibility had never occurred to me. I couldn't imagine anyone being homesick for the wilds of America. From what I had heard, it was almost beyond backward.

"Truthfully?"

"Yes, truthfully."

He nodded. "I miss it very much. It's much different— softer, in a way, greener, everything in abundance." He looked wistful.

"Then, why did you come here?" I asked. "I thought perhaps that your situation in America was . . . that perhaps you weren't quite . . . that maybe prosperity wasn't . . ." I stopped and gave it up.

He smiled. "They're quite right," he said. "You're the very picture of tact." He paused a moment. "No, financially, we were quite well off. My father died two years ago, leaving me to watch after my mother and sisters. I also have two brothers. They're both planters." He paused, as though he expected a comment.

"Very nice," I said, not really knowing what planters were. Farmers of some kind? "And were you a planter, too?"

He laughed aloud. "Lord, no. Couldn't stand it. I was always the one dashing off with some frontiersman or the other to explore. I wanted to see what was beyond the Shenandoahs, and then beyond the Mississippi. Quite some country there. I followed George Findley's and Benjamin Cutbirth's trail across the Cumberland Gap on into Boonesboro, then went to the Missouri Territory to see the old frontiersman named Daniel Boone who had founded Boonesboro.

He told me about some things farther west, and I went out there one year—all the way out to a place Boone had told me about where the earth bubbles up near the Yellowstone River.'' He stopped, not seeing anything except his memories. "You'd have to see that to believe it, Frankie. I'd like to take you there sometime.''

I thought here I might get an answer to another question that had been on my mind. "Wouldn't Nancy mind?'' I was very offhand.

He glanced up at me sharply. "Nancy? How did you know about Nancy?''

I felt myself go red. "You mentioned her name while you were delirious.''

He laughed. "Capital! I called out for Nancy! What in the world did I say?''

"Just that she was sweet, or something like that.'' I was embarrassed and couldn't look at him.

"That she is,'' he said carefully. "And about your question, no, Nancy wouldn't mind. I'm sure she'd love to have you along. She always goes with me, and she's one for company.''

I waited for more, but he said nothing. "It sounds interesting,'' I finally said. "You sound almost as though you plan to go back there. But,'' I added, "you still haven't told me why you decided to come here.''

He smiled at me again. "I do plan to go back someday. This place,'' he glanced around the library, "is almost too quiet. Too boring. Too . . .'' he paused, groping for a word. "Too *settled*.''

"Of course it's settled,'' I said a little impatiently. "It's been settled since before the Romans were here.''

"Ah, yes. You'd have a devil of a time trying to find Roman ruins in Tennessee. You might try for some Indian mounds, or even, if the tales the Indians tell are to be believed, the remains of the Spanish who trekked through there a long time ago.''

"I'll just stay here and search for Roman relics,'' I said. "Now, as to why—''

He held up a hand to keep me from saying it. "I'm getting there, Frankie. Don't rush me.'' He leaned up in his chair and put his elbows on the edge of the chess table. "I suppose I came because I felt obligated. My father always told me about this place when I was young. He left under something of a cloud, you know, and even though he made his mark in Virginia, he always regarded this place as his real home. I heard about Foxcroft from the time I was old enough to walk. He even named our plantation Fox Haven. At any rate, when he died, I inherited Fox Haven, although I didn't particularly want it. My younger brother, George, really ran it. When Banks came to visit me..."

I was so astonished that I interrupted him. "Banks visited you? Good heavens, I thought the man exerted himself if he had to write a letter. I'm amazed."

He leaned back again. "Yes, Banks actually looked me up. He's a sharp one, you know—a regular Philadelphia lawyer."

This was something new. "What's a Philadelphia lawyer?"

"A sharp, slick talker," he said. "Someone like Banks. Your father really knew what he was doing when he put the estate in the hands of a solicitor like Banks."

"True," I said. "I didn't mean to interrupt you. You were telling me about why you came here." I waited pointedly.

"I'm getting there," he grumbled. "At any rate, when Banks came to Fox Haven and told me that I was the only one left to inherit Foxcroft, I told him definitely not, in no uncertain terms. Then he said it would be sold and the rest of the family would be turned out."

"Banks said *that?*" I hadn't had the vaguest clue.

Wykeham nodded. "He said it was my duty to come over here and see to things, and take the responsibility of the family."

"And what did you say?"

"I told him I already had enough responsibility at Fox Haven. I had the plantation, my brothers, my mother, and my sisters. I didn't want any more."

I nodded. "Then what?"

"He said it was my duty, and then my mother chimed in and said it was my duty, then George offered to take full responsibility for Fox Haven and my family there. I didn't have much of an out, so I agreed to come over here." He grinned at me. "Aside from my unusual welcome, I do like it here, but I admit that the thought of returning is always at the back of my mind."

"I'd hate to see you leave," I said, surprising myself. I think I surprised Wykeham, as well. "Really?" he asked. I nodded yes and turned to the chessboard. "We'd better postpone our game," I said, to cover my feelings. "I need to return to Dower House and get Babs ready to go to London with Lizzie."

"So you've relented on that point?"

I nodded. "You're partially responsible for that," I told him. "Do you remember that you took Babs's side when I mentioned it? You said it would do her good to go to the city and meet other people."

"I do think so, but I didn't mean to be telling you what to do."

I glanced at him. "You're officially Babs's guardian, since you're the earl. I was merely following your wishes."

He looked at me, then laughed. "You're using me for an excuse, you wretch. If you hadn't decided yourself to let her go, every word I've ever said wouldn't have changed your mind."

I stood. "I fail to see what's so funny," I snapped.

Wykeham was still shaking with laughter as I stalked out of the library and sent for the carriage to take me back to the Dower House. Now that he was on the mend, the man was impossible.

It took forever to get Babs and Lizzie on their way to London. Babs had chattered nonstop from the moment she knew she was going. We decided that Mademoiselle DeSalle would accompany her as something of chaperone, although Lizzie assured me that Babs would never be out of her sight. Knowing Lizzie and Babs as I did, I doubted that, and insisted on Mademoiselle. She wasn't much, but she was better than nothing. Besides, Mademoiselle was overjoyed to be going, prattling on about "ze balls, ze routs, ze wonderful sights." I decided I should have to go to London soon myself to check on Babs, but I didn't mention it to

Lizzie, since she considered herself quite matronly and able to see after both Babs and Mademoiselle. After all, she told me, thinking she was rubbing salt into the wound, *she* was a married woman.

I think the whole household breathed a sigh of relief when the carriages rolled down the drive. Even the timid Clara ventured that she was sure things would be quiet from now on around the Dower House. Then she went off, book under her arm, with Charlie to look for rabbits so they could train Charlie's dog. Annie decided to go with them, and that left me alone at last. With a sigh of relief, I found Griggins and walked out to the field to plan my dig. Imagine my delight when I came upon Pembroke, standing there looking quite sour.

"Foolishness, if you ask me," he muttered.

"Now, Mr. Pembroke, you're merely irritated because you've lost your field for the season. You can certainly plant it when I've finished." I was quite charitable, considering I had won.

Pembroke gave me a mutinous look. "The earl was daft from all that sickness. I'm sure he'll change his mind when he sees how a perfectly good field is going to waste with you digging holes all over it." He turned on his heel. "Good day," he said, not even looking at me.

"Good day, Mr. Pembroke," I called cheerily after him. "I'll let you know when I've finished."

Griggins and I spent a very satisfactory afternoon setting grids for some trenches.

After Babs had gone, my days fell into a very pleasurable pattern. I hadn't realized the child had been so disruptive to the household. Clara usually gave lessons in the morning, then went off somewhere exploring with Annie and Charlie. I spent the mornings after the dew had dried off digging my trenches. I was getting along very well, and seemed to have uncovered the corner of a villa. It was very exciting, and I had to force myself to go slowly. I wanted to spend the entire day every day, but felt I owed it to Wykeham to spend afternoons with him. Finally, I cut my time there down to an hour or two a day. Wykeham was progressing marvelously and really didn't need my company. He was even getting around outside now.

One day, to my surprise, I looked around at the digs and there he stood. I was not at my most fastidious, of course, since I had been down on my hands and knees sifting dirt while Griggins dug. I shoved my hair back with a grimy hand, and attempted to straighten my dress, only to make two long dirt streaks on it with my hands. Wykeham laughed. "You're only making it worse," he said. "I don't mind the dirt at all."

"Good," I said, hopping over a trench and a mound of dirt. "What are you doing here? Have you taken to walking this far?"

"Yes." He leaned on his cane. "I wanted to see for myself what Pembroke's been grumbling about. He tells me you're ruining his field."

"*His* field! The man has no sensitivity at all! He'd have cabbages growing on the cathedral grounds if he could."

Wykeham laughed. "I have to agree. I did tell him he could have his field back in a year or two, when you finished with it. He wasn't happy about that."

I grinned. "I imagine not. I'd have loved to have seen his face then."

Wykeham grinned back. "You and Pembroke don't seem to be best friends." He glanced at my trenches. "Would you show me what you're doing?"

I hesitated, and Wykeham caught it. "If you'd rather not, I understand."

"It isn't that," I said. "It's just that I'm rather defensive about this. Most people don't think digging for artifacts is suitable for a woman to do."

He looked at me gravely. "I assure you I'm not one of them."

I looked right into those turquoise eyes. They were looking right through me and I caught my breath. "I'd love to show you," I said, reaching for his hand to help him over the piles of dirt. He took my fingers in a warm clasp, and followed me slowly up to the trenches, leaning somewhat heavily on his cane.

As he looked at our day's booty—a shard of pottery and

three metal lumps that I had decided were two coins and part of a buckle—he seemed impressed. He even felt the metal, commenting that it was amazing that something that old could survive. He also looked down into our trenches while I explained the methods of digging to uncover the layers of occupation. We had only a corner of the mosaic showing, but it promised to be quite complete.

He smiled at me when I ran out of breath after explaining what we were doing. "I take it you're an enthusiast," he said. "I've never seen you so excited about anything else."

I stopped and remembered the reaction my enthusiasm usually generated. "I'm sorry," I said, quite icily. "I forgot everyone doesn't approve."

"Oh, but I do approve, and quite heartily," he said quickly, looking at me. "I think it's wonderful that you can find something this old and rare."

"Really?" It was hardly original, but I was too amazed to think of anything else to say.

Wykeham laughed. "Yes, really. But then, I've always thought you were a remarkable woman."

I was speechless, then I reacted in a totally uncharacteristic way. I blushed, then I stammered like a tongue-tied miss. "Thank you."

"No need to thank me—I meant it." He shifted his weight and his cane went into the soft earth.

"Are you all right?" I asked quickly, noting his pallor for the first time. "Have you overdone yourself?"

"Perhaps a little," he said, beginning to make his way out of the field. "Do you think Griggins would mind going for a cart?"

I motioned to Griggins, but he was already out of the field, on his way. Griggins, like the rest of the household, had been charmed by the earl. "I'll have you home in jig time," he said gruffly. "You just sit and rest here until I get back." He took off at a lope.

I sat down beside Wykeham to wait. "You shouldn't have—" I began, but he interrupted me.

"Don't fuss," he said with a smile. "You sound just like my sisters. I'll be fine."

"I don't think so. You shouldn't have—"

He interrupted me again, obviously paying no attention to what I was saying. "What are you going to do with your discovery once you've finished your excavations? Surely you're planning to write this up in some scholarly journal."

"That's not funny."

He glanced at me in surprise. "I apologize. I didn't mean to be humorous. I think something this important should be presented to the world in some way. Perhaps a paper to a society or something?"

I grimaced. This was a very sore point with me. "I'll probably never be able to present anything unless I can get some man of my acquaintance to read a paper about my findings to the Society of Antiquaries."

"A man? Why? Wouldn't it be better if you presented it yourself?"

"Females are not allowed," I said grimly. "Evidently, we're all supposed to stay at home and tend to our knitting, or whatever."

He didn't say anything for a moment. Then he spoke, and his voice was full of surprise. "That's amazing. Could you go in disguise?"

"I hadn't thought about that," I said, imagining myself in breeches, addressing that august group. Since I'm not exactly slender across the bosom, I doubted I could carry it off.

Wykeham dismissed the idea before I did. "Forget that," he said. "It would never work, and besides, you shouldn't have to disguise yourself to present your work." He sat a moment, frowning. "I'll tell you what—I'll do it for you. The condition is that you have to sign your own name to the paper. Then I'll go in there and read it."

"You?"

He looked at me. "Certainly, me. Or wouldn't the exalted Society of Antiquaries allow the earl of Wykeham to present a paper?"

"Of course they would. They'd be delighted."

"Then, what's the problem?"

I smiled broadly. "There isn't any. Oh, that's wonderful! You don't know how much this means to me!" I grabbed his hands and held them. He looked at me and smiled, catching

me with those turquoise eyes. Suddenly I felt quite giddy—
whether from his eyes, or from happiness at having an offer
to present my findings, I didn't know. It was a very pleasant
sensation. He kept looking at me and I felt myself being
drawn to him. I leaned a little closer to him, and it seemed
to me that he moved toward me.

"Here you are, my lord." It was Griggins, returning with
a great crashing of brush as he brought the cart around the
curve. "Told you I'd be here in a trice." He hopped down
and reached for Wykeham as I hastily stood up and moved
away. "And look who I've brought along."

"Hello, you two," Harry said as he rode up behind the
cart and dismounted. "Whatever are you doing out here?
Glad to see you up and around, Wykeham." He extended a
hand to help the earl into the cart.

"And Frankie." He turned to me with a smile that rapidly
faded as he took in my somewhat mussed appearance. "Did
you fall, Frankie?" he asked, puzzled.

"Lady Frances has been showing me her excavations,"
Wykeham explained.

"Oh, that," Harry said, glancing at the field. "Thought
you'd finished with all this twaddle, Frankie." He turned
and gave the earl one of those infuriating looks men sometimes exchange. "Women do get these queer notions, don't
they?" he said.

To the earl's credit, he didn't answer, but then, he really
didn't get a chance to. I was up in the boughs in an instant.
"Really, Harry," I sputtered, trying to remain calm. "You
knew about my excavations. I told you what I was doing
here."

"To be sure, you did, my darlin'," he said with a grin.
"And if you remember, I told you that you'd soon have me
to occupy your time."

I glanced at Wykeham. His face was pale and set, and he
was staring from Harry to me and back again. "If the two
of you will excuse me," he said carefully, "I must be
getting back to Foxcroft. I'm afraid I've done too much
already."

"Of course," Harry said. "Frankie and I were just

leaving, as well. Thought we might go for a ride," he said, finally including me in his plans.

"Harry, I have things to do here." I hoped my voice was icy.

He looked around. "What? Surely you aren't about to dabble in the dirt."

"I am." I said firmly. "I never leave here without covering my trenches and getting ready for the next day. That's very important."

"I can't see why. It's just one pile of dirt or another." Harry squinted as he looked over the mounds of dirt.

"No matter, Harry. I intend to finish here. Now."

Harry gave Wykeham another look and rolled his eyes heavenward. Wykeham evidently sensed a contretemps, as he promptly invited Harry over for some refreshment. Harry quickly accepted. I was quite out of charity with him as they rode off, leaving Griggins to finish helping me.

When I walked back up to the trenches, I made a conscious effort to put Harry's remarks out of my mind. Why his attitude bothered me, I didn't know, because he had made no bones about thinking my work was all frivolity. With great effort I concentrated on showing Griggins where to cover things. It didn't work. Angry with Harry, I did what most people would do—I snapped at Griggins instead. To his everlasting credit, he said not a word.

By the time we had finished, I had worked off most of my anger, and had even mentioned to Griggins that I might have been somewhat short with him. He merely grunted, making me feel my magnanimous gesture was wasted. But, by this time I was already mentally composing the paper that Wykeham had promised to read. I had always dreamed of having my work presented to the Society of Antiquaries, but I knew that as a female, I would face the same kind of ridicule that Harry had shown. At least Wykeham had had the courtesy not to laugh. Indeed, he was interested.

I pushed Harry's remarks out of my mind and concentrated on my paper, and I was unbelievably exhilarated as Griggins and I walked home.

Chapter 9

I had expected Harry that night—possibly even as a guest for supper. However, supper time came and went, as well as a very dull evening spent playing cards with Clara Conroy after the children had supposedly gone to sleep. Noises from upstairs indicated otherwise, but I didn't care to go up. At last poor Clara, after many looks at the ceiling whenever something crashed above, left me and went upstairs, her book under her arm.

Alone, I had a small fire built to take the evening chill and sat in the library reading a letter that had just arrived from Lizzie. As I was frowning over Lizzie's news, Jervis announced Harry. Jervis obviously did not approve of such late visitors, as his voice quivered with indignation. "Lord Harry Apsley," he said frostily, then lowered his voice. "Shall I inform him that you are not available for visitors?"

Before I could answer, Harry, whistling quite cheerfully, ignored manners and came wandering in beside Jervis. I was sorry to note that he was a trifle bosky.

"How ye doin', Frankie?" he asked in a slurred voice, collapsing into the nearest chair and stretching his legs out to the fire. "Chilly out tonight, and that little fire feels good. You certainly know how to make a man feel welcome." He smiled lopsidedly at me.

"I think we need some coffee, Jervis," I said to the butler's frozen and horrified countenance. "Hurry, if you please."

"Certainly." Jervis bit the word off like a bullet and left.

I put up my letter. "I didn't expect you this late, Harry," I said. "I'm surprised Wykeham let you out in such a condition."

"I'm not so bad," Harry said with another smile. "In

fact, I've been much worse, and as for Wykeham, he wasn't quite the thing—his outing today left him the worse for wear—so I convinced him to go on to bed early in the evening. He invited me to stay and then left me downstairs with a bottle or two.''

"Obviously, Wykeham doesn't know you very well."

Harry laughed. "Well enough. He's coming to our wedding, you know. I invited him."

I stared at him. "Harry, there is no wedding—at least, not now. You know we have a wager on that, and I fully expect to win."

"As do I, my pet," he said, just as Jervis came in with coffee. Jervis gave Harry an icy look and set the tray down between us on a table. He hovered around, acting as if he were ready to pounce on Harry, until I dismissed him.

I got two cups of coffee down Harry before very much else was said. "That demmed stuff is bitter," Harry finally sputtered, downing the last of the cupful. In truth, it did seem to be a trifle strong. I supposed Jervis was trying to do as much for me as possible.

"Are you feeling better?" I asked.

"No," he growled, shaking his head. "I felt much better before you started me on this stuff. Nothing wrong with feeling a little, um . . .''

"Drunk."

"Hardly. I've been drunk before, and I can tell you for a fact that I'm not drunk. I am out of sorts."

I was foolish enough to walk right into it. "Why?"

"Because of you, Frankie." He put his cup down and leaned over to me, pushing the table out of the way and grasping my hands in his. "I'm absolutely mad about you, don't you know that? And you keep putting me off."

I pulled my hands away. "Please, Harry, this is not the time or the place for such a conversation."

"Then, dammit, tell me when the time and place is. I can't wait forever, Frankie." He stood, paced over to the fireplace, and leaned against the mantel. He looked devilishly handsome standing there, the fire flickering on his features.

"I have responsibilities," I began. "I want to finish my excavations, and then there are the girls. I have to see to them."

Harry shook his head. "No, you don't. They're the earl's problem."

"I'd hardly call them a problem," I said stiffly.

He moved over next to me. "You know what I meant," he said testily. "The earl is their guardian, not you. Besides, they don't need you, and I do."

I looked up at him. "It doesn't matter whether the earl is their guardian or not, Harry. They're *my* sisters, and I'm still morally responsible for them. For instance, Lizzie wrote me just today that she fears Babs has fallen in love with someone. Just how could I go to the earl with such a trifle?"

"Babs?" Harry was instantly alert and sat back down across from me. "Just what does Lizzie have to say?"

"You don't have to be concerned, Harry."

He reached for my hands again, but gently this time. "I want to be, Frankie. Whatever bothers you is a problem of mine. I want to help you."

I was quite overcome. "Oh, Harry," I said, suddenly dribbling tears like a watering pot. I was quite ashamed of myself, but when Harry reached over to hold me, it was a very good feeling.

"Now, hush that. You know you can confide in me, sweetheart," he said, mopping my eyes and putting away his handkerchief.

"Oh, it's probably nothing—you know how dramatic Babs is. Lizzie simply writes that Babs is walking around like a lovestruck calf and throwing out all kinds of hints about having a *parti* and getting married before long. Lizzie has no idea who it might be and swears to me that she's had Babs chaperoned every second. Of course, with Mademoiselle as a chaperone, that doesn't mean very much."

Harry laughed. "It's wonderful that you told me, because I can set your fears to rest. I've seen Mademoiselle DeSalle and Babs in London, and I can assure you that Mademoiselle is practically a dragon when it comes to Babs. She's probably afraid you'll turn her off without a reference if anything happened to Babs." He moved closer and I noted that he hadn't removed his arm from my shoulder. I really didn't want him to—it felt quite comfortable there. Harry continued, "I did see Babs in the park with Lizzie one day and they were walking with a young man. I didn't remark him except to note that he had spots. That's probably the person Babs fancies herself in love with." He gave me his smile. "As I recall from my advanced years, young girls have a tendency to do that sort of thing."

I smiled back at him. "You're quite right, Harry. I'm foolish to be worried about it. I imagine Babs will fall in love a hundred times before she gets around to marrying someone."

"Most girls do," Harry said. There was a pause, and I thought he was going to kiss me, but he moved away a little and spoke instead. "By the way, is Babs well fixed on her dowry?" Seeing my shocked expression, he hastily added, "Not that I'm prying, but I do know that the earl doesn't have the access to the *ton* that I do, and I thought I might be able to throw a few suggestions his way."

"I understand, Harry, and thank you. It's very kind of you to think about us."

He smiled again and took my hands. "I told you, whatever concerns you also concerns me. Now, about Babs—"

I shrugged. "Papa left her quite well fixed, and she has some money from her mother, as well. Her mother was an only child, so her income was sizable."

"Splendid," Harry said, "but we'll have to watch out for fortune hunters, won't we? I'll keep the idea in the back of my mind, and introduce her around to some eligible young men."

"I hardly think we need to try to marry her off. Actually, as scatterbrained as Babs is, she needs to wait to marry until she learns some sense—say five and twenty or so."

Harry laughed again. "And you, you're five and twenty— do you think you're ready now?"

I was ready for a sharp remark, but when Harry looked at me, I felt myself blush. "I don't know," I finally stammered, but then Harry leaned over close to me and kissed me. As I had anticipated, it was quite wonderful. Whatever faults Harry had, kissing certainly wasn't one. I was quite breathless when he finally lifted his head.

"Will you marry me, Frankie?" he whispered, holding

me close to him. I could feel his heart beating against my own.

"Harry," I said, groping for words and still trying to catch my breath. I wanted to say yes and he knew it. "Say you'll marry me, Frankie," he murmured against my hair. "We need each other. We always have."

"I want to marry you, Harry," I began, "but . . ."

Harry didn't wait for me to finish. "I knew it! I knew you would!" He looked down at me and smiled broadly. "I won't even hold you to our wager, my sweet. For this, I'll gladly pay you your guinea." His head lowered and he kissed me again, quite effectively disrupting my thinking. My head was spinning, and I was quite lost as Harry moved his mouth over mine, catching my lip in his teeth and teasing the corners of my mouth.

"Harry," I gasped, as he kissed me under my ear, giving me gooseflesh. "Harry, please—"

"Mmmmm. Please what, my love? Just tell me." He kissed my throat and chuckled as I shuddered.

I forced myself to pull away from him. Where I got the strength to do it, I had no idea, because I wanted nothing more than to stay right there and respond to Harry. He had awakened the strangest, most exquisite feelings I had ever experienced, but I simply *had* to speak to him. "Harry," I said firmly, although somewhat shakily, "please. I need to say something."

"You've already said everything I need to hear," he murmured, reaching for me again.

I grasped his wrists and held him. "Harry, please. You didn't let me finish what I was saying. I want to marry you, Harry, really I do, but I need to finish my work."

"Your work?" He was quite blank. "Oh, you mean your digging." A harsh look came over his face. "Do you mean to tell me that you're going to continue with that drivel? Of all the stupid, idiotic . . ."

I felt tears come behind my eyes. "I told you that I have the girls, Harry, and that I want to finish excavating the field. I don't want to get married until everything is settled."

"And when will that be?" he asked bitterly, walking away from me toward the fireplace. "Once you get your dirt moved, you'll have to wait until the girls are married—what will that be, ten years or so? Then, I'm sure you'll have to wait until Wykeham gets married off and ensures the succession." He walked to me and grabbed me by the shoulders. "I won't wait forever on you, Frankie—do you hear me! You're not the only woman in the world, you know."

The tears fell in earnest now. "Harry, you don't understand."

"Oh, I understand all right. *You're* the one who doesn't understand. And I tell you this, Frankie, I'll never be shackled to some chit who thinks more of her family and a pile of old pottery than she does of me."

"I care for you, Harry. I really do. You know that."

"All I know is that you're dangling me like a fish on a string, Frankie. And something else I know is that I don't have to put up with it." With that, he turned and went out of the library, slamming the door behind him.

"Harry," I said, listening to the echo of the door in the quiet house. Then I sat down in the chair and put my face in my hands. I looked up at a noise, thinking Harry had returned. It would be just like him to be so enraged, then come back apologizing, but it was only Jervis. "Is everything all right, Lady Frances?" he asked stiffly, looking quite pointedly at my ravaged face.

I turned away from him. "Quite all right, Jervis. You may go on to bed now." There was a long silence, then I heard him leave the library and shut the door softly. I sat and stared at the dying fire for a long time. I realized that Harry wasn't coming back.

I slept in late the next morning, and when I awoke, I saw that I looked terrible. My face was all swollen and puffy, and there were large, purplish-black circles under my eyes. I was not a lovely sight. Still, I felt I had to do something. Harry had mentioned that the earl had invited him to stay the night, and I decided perhaps I should go to Foxcroft and try to talk with him. I didn't intend to grovel or apologize, but I felt I should try to explain my reasons. But I certainly didn't want to go face Harry when I looked as if I were suffering from the plague, so I decided to wait until late afternoon. Surely, I would look better then. What I needed was a brisk morning at my digs.

Actually, I spent more than the morning. Griggins and I were working hard and had uncovered more of the floor. I was beginning to see the outlines of the villa, and while it wasn't a very large one, it was classically shaped. Evidently, the mosaics I had uncovered were part of the atrium. I carefully sketched each thing and labeled it with notes as to where and how it had been discovered. We were getting quite a little hoard of pottery shards as well.

Griggins came up to me after we had been working for what I thought was a fairly short time. "Lady Frankie, do you want to stop to eat? I don't want to complain, but I'm fair famished."

"Nonsense, Griggins," I said. "It couldn't be time for nuncheon." I fumbled in my skirts for my pocket watch and flipped it open. "See, Griggins," I began, then stopped as I saw it was past three o'clock. "Good heavens," I said. "Griggins, why didn't you tell me it was so late? I wanted to go over to Foxcroft, and it'll be almost too late by the time we get all this covered. Really, Griggins, you should keep up with the time."

Griggins rolled his eyes at me—a most disconcerting habit he has—and mumbled.

"What, Griggins? I can't understand you."

He leaned over and spoke slowly and distinctly. "I said why don't you go on, and I'll go back and get cook to fix me some nuncheon. Then I'll come back here and cover everything."

"Really, Griggins, you don't have to shout. I'm not deaf, you know." I looked around the digs and then up at the sky. It was cloudless. "Very well, Griggins, that's a very good idea. We'll both go back to the Dower House for nuncheon."

Without another word, Griggins threw down his trowel and stalked off toward the Dower House. I was really going to have to speak to him. He was getting quite out of hand.

It was past four when I finally got to Foxcroft Manor. Wykeham was walking around the garden when I arrived. "I'm surprised to see you up and around," I told him.

"Harry told me you were somewhat done in by your walk yesterday."

"I did do a little too much," he admitted, motioning for me to sit down beside him on a garden bench. I looked at him closely. He was much paler than usual, and there seemed to be lines around his eyes that I hadn't noticed before.

"Are you sure you're all right?" I asked. "You don't seem to be doing as well as you were."

He smiled at me. "I suppose I'll have to confess. I've already had quite a raking over by David, so you won't have to say anything. I decided to try a short ride yesterday morning, and then tried to walk away the pain. Unfortunately, neither the ride nor the walk was successful." He leaned slightly on his cane and a shadow of pain crossed his face. Impulsively, I reached over and covered his hand with mine. "I'm so sorry," I said, looking into his eyes.

He slowly pulled his hand away and forced a smile. "Thank you, but I assure you I'm fine. I'll get over this and be on the mend again."

What he had said finally hit me. "Ride? You tried to ride? Good heavens, you'll shake your wound open. Whatever were you thinking? Surely, you know better than . . ."

He interrupted me and held up his hand. "Please. I told you that David has already said everything necessary, and called me every name he could think of, as well. I could have supplied a few myself."

"All right, I won't mention it again." I bit my tongue on the other things I had to say, and instead turned casually to the subject of my visit. "Is Harry here? He said he was staying the night."

He looked at me, surprised. "No. I thought you knew he was going back to London this morning. As a matter of fact, he left so early that I almost missed him."

"Harry got up early?" That was news. He wasn't noted for being an early bird. He must have been furious with me.

Wykeham nodded. "He was out and headed for London by nine o'clock. I tried to get him to stay a few days, but he was quite out of sorts." He paused delicately. "I think that perhaps he might have had a headache."

"You mean, he drank too much last night."

"I really couldn't say that. I wasn't a very good host, I'm afraid. I went on to bed early, and left Harry to his own devices. He might have drunk more than usual."

Evidently, Wykeham didn't know that Harry had visited me late, and I certainly wasn't going to tell him. "No matter," I said, pretending Harry's departure was of no consequence. "I'll be going up to London soon, and I'll see Harry there, I'm sure."

Wykeham gave me a strange look. "Harry told me about your plans."

"My excavations? Wykeham, I'm so excited about it! I think I'm going to find the foundations of a complete villa. The atrium is particularly well marked. I've already jotted down some notes for my paper to the Society of Antiquaries."

Wykeham laughed aloud. "I'm delighted for you. But no, those weren't the plans I was thinking of. Harry told me that you and he are getting married very soon."

I felt myself go red and began to stammer. "We've discussed it, but that's a while away," I finally managed to say. "I have several things to do first."

"Oh, yes, your trip to London," he said. "One of my sisters was planning to be married two years ago, and there were shopping expeditions, frenzied weeks of sewing, cards to be sent, and a thousand other things to do. I didn't know getting married was so complicated."

"It does seem that way," I agreed. "Did she have a beautiful wedding? I've never cared for such ceremony myself."

He smiled at me. "No, I wouldn't think all those fripperies would be to your taste. As for Rebeckah, no, she had no wedding at all. Her husband-to-be and I were on a trip to Kentucky to do some surveying. We thought we'd go slightly north of the road Boone took through the Cumberland Mountains to save some time." He paused and looked devastated. "We were looking for a pass through the mountains, and we were on a cliff above some falls. Johnny lost his footing and fell—it must have been a hundred feet." Wykeham stopped and swallowed hard. "It took him two days to die," he said, almost in a whisper.

"I'm sorry." It sounded inadequate. "What did you do?"

"I buried him there where he died, went back home and told his family and Rebeckah what had happened, then hired someone to help me and went to Kentucky to finish our surveying." He had a sad note in his voice. "There was nothing else I could do."

"Of course." There was a long pause between us. "Did your sister recover?"

"Oh, yes. Rebeckah's a strong woman." He smiled at me and pulled a letter from his pocket. "It's strange that we should be talking about her. I received a letter from her just this morning and got a pleasant surprise. She's on her way here for a visit."

"How wonderful for you. Why did she decide to visit? Has she ever been here before? I'm sure she'll love it."

Wykeham held up a hand to stop me. "No more, Frankie, please." He laughed. "One of your most interesting traits is asking a dozen questions at a time. I don't know how you keep up with them."

"It's a gift," I said promptly.

He chuckled again as he returned Rebeckah's letter to his pocket. "I can't answer in order. No, she's never been here before, and I think she'll like it, but she'll probably like Virginia better. As to why she's coming, Perkins wrote them about my injury, and I think my dear sister needs to come satisfy herself that I'm not at death's door."

I looked at him critically. "Well, if you rest a great deal, you'll probably be in the bloom of health by the time she gets here."

"Not a chance," Wykeham said, leaning back and stretching his legs out in front of him. "She left shortly after she posted the letter. I expect her to get here sometime in the next fortnight." He looked at me and hesitated a moment. "Do you think I could ask a very great favor of you?"

"Of course." After what I had done to him, he could ask for the moon and I would try to get it.

"I need someone to see that the house is set to rights. Not Foxcroft—Mrs. Simms has done a wonderful job," he amended hastily, "but the London house."

"The London house?" I sat up straighter. I had almost

forgotten about the London house, since we seldom went up there. "Good heavens, there must be a foot of dust there!"

"I was afraid of that," he said ruefully. "Do you think . . ."

I resigned myself to my fate. "Of course I can," I said. "But do you think I might wait a week before I go up? I really need to see about the atrium, and it might start raining at any time."

"Take as long as you need," he said. "Rebeckah will stay here at Foxcroft for a while, and I'll take her up to London to see the sights later." He looked at me and smiled. "I certainly appreciate this. It's wonderful to have someone I can depend on, and perhaps since you're going there anyway to shop for finery and to see Harry, the trip won't be tedious for you."

"No." I stopped, distracted. There was the matter of Harry again, and then, there was Lizzie's letter. "I need to go to London fairly soon, at any rate," I told him. "I want to check on Babs."

"How's she getting on?" To my surprise, he seemed really interested.

I found myself telling him about Lizzie's letter. "Harry assures me that young girls fall in love a dozen times a day," I said, "so I hope it's nothing, but with Babs, one never knows."

"I'll have someone check, if it will make you feel better."

I smiled gratefully at him. "That won't be necessary, but thank you. I'll see her in a fortnight or so." I stood and held out a hand to him. "Let's go in now—and you can tell me if there are any special arrangements I can make for Rebeckah."

Chapter 10

I was busy for the next two weeks, seeing to Wykeham, to the Dower House, and to my excavations. I got up early each morning, then fell exhausted into bed at night. I didn't want Wykeham doing anything, since I hoped he would be in better health when his sister arrived. I decided that parts of Foxcroft should be painted and refurbished, and that was what was so difficult. In truth, my excavations suffered somewhat, but I felt I could invest more time in them as soon as I had run up to London and seen to the house and Babs. I finished at Foxcroft two days before Wykeham expected Rebeckah, and went on up to London. I was not as worried about Babs, as I had received another letter from Lizzie. It seemed that Babs had evidently either given up—or lost her true love—and had settled down. She was assiduously visiting museums and attending lectures, so Lizzie told me. I found this quite hard to credit, but then, miracles have been known to occur. I rather thought it was yet another role for Babs—the rejected heroine seeks refuge in the arts.

My trip to London was uneventful, but quite dirty, and I hoped the message I had sent to the London house had gotten there. All I wanted was a bath, some supper, and a clean bed. When we got there, the house was dark, so I sent Griggins to bang on the door. There had been only a minimum staff—Mr. Skelton and his wife, two people who were not my favorites. Still, I expected them to have the house in some semblance of order, and at least have a cold supper and the candles lit. After Griggins practically beat the door down, we decided there was only one course of action left for us—to break in. We went around back to break a window, but discovered someone had already had this idea. The window was broken, the door ajar, and the inside picked rather clean. The Skeltons were not to be seen.

"I always knew those two were not to be trusted," Griggins muttered, searching through drawers for tinder.

When he found some, and struck it, the light was bright enough for us to see that it would take major effort to ready the house. Griggins found some candles and placed them in the sconces, lighting the downstairs fairly well. I sent Katie upstairs to light the room there.

Evidently the Skeltons—or someone else—had hastily

decamped when my letter was received. It was still lying on the hall table, opened. The furniture was still in place, but the pictures, silver, linens, and some of the books were gone. They had taken all the things easily carried. There were linens on the beds, and I sent Griggins to an inn for something to eat. We would then try to get a night's sleep before we did anything else. I dreaded writing Wykeham with the news.

The next morning, the first thing I did was write to Wykeham and ask him if he wanted me to refurbish the house. I couldn't wait for the mails, so I sent John the coachman back to Foxcroft with the letter and instructions to wait for an answer. I thought he could be back day after tomorrow, which would give me time to inventory the losses, and perhaps even visit Lizzie and see about Babs.

I also sent a note to Lizzie about the house, then settled down to see what had been taken. There had been a list of the furnishings in Papa's papers in the library, and this proved invaluable, but it was still far from complete. Even a cursory glance showed me that the Skeltons, or whoever was in league with them, had managed to take a great deal. They had even taken some silver belonging to my mother that I had meant to take to the Dower House. It wasn't that valuable to anyone except myself, but I hated to see it lost.

The knocker boomed just as I was finishing my inspection of the downstairs. It was Lizzie and Babs. "A robbery!" Babs breathed. "How very exciting! Did you see who did it, Frankie?"

"Of course not," I said, leading the way to the small breakfast room where we could sit and have some tea. "I wrote them I was coming, so they took everything they could before I arrived."

"You shouldn't have written them," Babs said. "Then you could have caught them red-handed. How utterly romantic!"

"Bosh!" I snorted. "I thought you were out of that stage, Babs. If I had come in and caught them red-handed, they most likely would have bashed my head in."

She looked at me gravely. "Oh, no, Frankie, that's not how it would have been. You would have been a heroine.

You might have been wounded just a little bit, a bruise or such—just enough to have to call someone. David, perhaps."

"David wouldn't come to London for a bruise," I said, sipping my tea.

"If he loved you, he would." Babs waved her hands melodramatically and looked anguished—obviously, something she had picked up straight out of Drury Lane.

"Nonsense. Besides, David and I are friends. He doesn't love me in that sense." I turned to Lizzie. "I thought you were taking her around to museums and whatever to get these maggoty romantic notions out of her head. I suppose she's been haunting the library and getting all those novels to read?"

"She has been going to museums," Lizzie said defensively, "and I certainly can't watch everything she reads, now, can I?"

"Just listen to the two of you," Babs cried, giving a very creditable shriek of agony. "Sitting there and talking about me as if I weren't even here. I'm perfectly capable of taking charge of my own life, and I don't need the two of you to tell me what to do."

I glanced up at her. She was pacing the floor. "Babs, please sit down," I said quite calmly. "Lizzie and I are responsible for you, no matter what you think."

Babs sat down with a petulant look on her face. "No, you're not," she said. "The earl is my guardian, and he's the only one who can tell me what to do."

"We don't need to bother Wykeham with our problems," I said briskly. "He has enough on his plate as it is."

"Thanks to you," Babs said with a snide smirk.

I glared at her. "That's enough, Barbara. Do you want to come back to the Dower House with me? I think perhaps London has gone to your head."

Babs threw herself at my feet and put her hands in a prayerful position to implore me. "Oh, please, please, Frankie, not that! Please let me stay—I beg of you!"

"Oh, for heaven's sake, Babs, will you get up?" I stood and rather unceremoniously jerked her upright. "It's precisely this that makes me think you don't need to be in London."

"I'll behave, Frankie, you know that. I'll be a perfect pattern card, I promise."

I gave up for the time being. "Very well, Babs. I have this house to ready for the earl and his sister, and I really don't have time for this right now. Plan on staying with Lizzie for a little longer." I paused a moment. "But don't think this gives you any leeway for misbehavior. If Lizzie even so much as *hints* that you have given her cause for worry, I'll have you right back at the Dower House."

Babs gave me a surly look. "Only Wykeham can order me about," she said. Then, at my scowl, she thought the better of her remarks. "I truly will behave, Frankie. You won't regret this."

"I hope not," I said shortly, and gave Lizzie a significant look. Sometimes Lizzie was as scatterbrained as Babs. "Now, I need to go shopping to get some prices in case the earl wants me to replace some of the things taken. Do you two want to go with me?"

They chorused "yes" together, and I quickly dressed and called for the carriage. Griggins had to drive us and wasn't too happy about that, but then, Griggins was always grumbling about something.

I had gotten the replacement items for the house ready to order and had interviewed for some new servants by the time I got Wykeham's letter telling me to proceed as I thought fit. I knew that was what he would do, but preferred his seal on the matter. He also told me that Rebeckah had now arrived at Foxcroft, and the two of them planned to stay there for at least a fortnight before coming up to London. That left me very little time to do what I needed to.

The next two weeks were sheer madness. I hired new servants, had painters and plasterers in, purchased new drapes, and, in general, redid the house. It looked quite fine, I thought, considering the short amount of time I had had. The new silver wasn't quite what I had wanted, but I had had to take what was available. The robbers had cleaned out the butler's pantry, and if Wykeham was to entertain, or even to eat, he had to have some silver. The Skeltons, or whoever the robbers were, had known exactly what to take that would convert easily to cash. I had taken it on myself to visit the Bow Street Runners and put them on the trail of our stolen property. I didn't think Wykeham would mind.

There was another complication, as well. After I had been in residence for the better part of a week, Harry came to see me. I had just settled in the new butler and housekeeper, an altogether unremarkable and somewhat nervous couple from Somerset, and Harry was the first visitor that Pinchbeck announced.

"Are you at home, milady?" Pinchbeck asked, after giving me Harry's somewhat ornate card. The butler looked significantly at the painters and plasterers surrounding me in the drawing room.

"Send him in, please," I said, trying in vain to tidy my hair. I might be on the outs with Harry, but I still wished to look somewhat presentable. I followed Pinchbeck to the door.

"Ah, there you are, my lovely," Harry said, rushing past Pinchbeck and crushing me in a hug, then planting a kiss right on my forehead. Pinchbeck stared at us, aghast. "I've missed you."

I felt myself go red. "Please, Harry. Let's go in here." I led him into the breakfast room and shut the door. I turned to speak to him, but before I could utter a sound, he caught me and kissed me soundly, and needless to add, quite expertly. "Oh, Frankie, you're so sweet," he mumbled against my skin. "My dear, sweet Frankie."

With great effort, I moved away from him. "I thought you were angry with me, Harry," I said, confused. "You left for London in such a huff."

He chuckled and gave me his smile. "Oh, Frankie, you know how I am. I was, I confess, a little overset, but I'm over it now, my sweet, and I would have been here days ago if I had known you were here. I just found out from Lizzie and Babs, so I wasted no time in coming to see you." He reached for me again, and I dodged.

"Really, Harry. This is not the time or the place. I'm having to see to the entire house before Wykeham and his sister come up."

Harry looked a little petulant and released me, propping himself against the door. "And why should you have to do this? The earl has enough money to hire someone to come up here and open the house. God knows, he's as rich as Croesus.''

"Hardly," I said dryly. "Don't forget that I kept the account books for Papa. The estate is quite solvent, but I'd hardly call the earl as rich as Croesus. Comfortable, perhaps.''

"All right, all right." Harry strode over to the windows and looked out. "I find it difficult to imagine what life would be like with money." He looked back at me and his voice was bitter. "No one knows how much my father likes to keep me on a short leash. He has plenty of blunt for everyone except me.''

"I didn't realize that, Harry. I thought you and your father were well on the way to making up your differences." I felt so for him that I went to him and put my hand on his arm.

"We have, to a point. He still likes to control the purse strings, though." He put his hand on mine and smiled down at me. "That, thank God, will soon be a thing of the past. But now, let's talk about you and me. I apologize for my behavior the last time I saw you. Could we begin again?" He looked so boyish and engaging as he looked at me that I couldn't refuse.

"There's no need to ask me, Harry. Of course, I forgive you—as I recall, you were a trifle, um, bosky."

He laughed and held me in his arms. "A trifle, perhaps, but more than a trifle in love with you." He looked at me a moment and then kissed me. "Frankie," he murmured, "please marry me. I need you so much." He kissed me again, holding me with one arm while the other hand traced patterns over my arm and shoulder and up my throat. It was the strangest, giddiest feeling. I felt I had no control over myself. "Say you'll marry me, Frankie."

"Yes," I mumbled, in spite of myself, enjoying all these new and strange feelings thoroughly. "Yes, Harry." I moved closer to him and put my hands on the back of his neck.

Instead of holding me closer, he shoved me backwards and held me by my shoulders. "Yes! You said yes! Frankie, you've made me the happiest man in London. In the whole world! I'm going right now and tell my father. He'll get in touch with Wykeham as soon as possible and we'll make the arrangements right away. We'll even do this by special license, if we can. I don't want to have to wait, sweetheart.'' He kissed me soundly again, picked up his gloves and hat, and was out the door before I could utter a single sound.

As soon as Pinchbeck closed the door behind him, I sank down into the nearest chair. What had I done? I had promised to marry Harry—not later, not after six months, but right now. And Harry didn't want to wait, so there would be no putting this off. Now I would never get my villa excavated. I would never write my paper for Wykeham to present to the Society of Antiquaries. At this moment that should be so happy, I burst into bitter tears.

———— Chapter 11 ————

It took me the better part of an hour to begin thinking straight again, but I finally composed myself. Here I was, crying over something I could fix. I merely had to be firm with Harry and tell him I had to wait. After all, it usually took several months to make arrangements, get a trousseau, and so on. I would have plenty of time. I hurried into the library and dashed off a note to Harry, telling him I needed to see him right away. That done, I watched as the drawing room got the finishing touches and then went upstairs to supervise the new draperies in what would be Rebeckah's room. I was doing it all in blue and cream. I hoped she would like it.

Harry, ever the gallant, answered my summons, but not until late afternoon, two days later. I had dressed and waited for him after I had written, but he hadn't appeared. I wrote again, and waited again. I wrote yet a third time, more than a little sharp, and waited once more. I determined to go find him if he didn't show up. I had the house all but completed, and wanted to go back home to work on my digs while the weather held. I had wasted enough time already. By the time he got there and Pinchbeck announced him, I was in quite a pelter.

"And what do you ask of me, my sweet?" Harry said, sweeping into the library and taking me into his arms.

"Actually, Harry, I had asked that you come to see me two days ago," I said, pulling away before he could kiss me. I knew from past experience that I needed to say what I wished before he began that. I would be as lost as I had been in the breakfast room.

Harry appeared astonished. "Frankie, darling, I wish I had known! You know I would have been here immediately." He took my hands and aimed for a kiss on my lips, but I dodged and he gave me a peck on the side of the head. "What's the matter, darling? On the outs with me? It won't happen again, I promise. I was out of town for a day or two, conferring with my father. He's delighted with our news, by the way."

I retreated behind a chair to put some distance between us. "That's what I needed to see you about, Harry. I simply can't marry you now."

His face changed—the smile faded and was replaced by a sharp, cold look. "What?" he snapped. "Just what are you telling me, Frankie? Are you crying off before we even announce anything?"

"No, not really, Harry," I began, but he interrupted me.

The sunny smile returned. "Then there's no problem, darling."

"Yes, there is, Harry." I took a deep breath. "I can't marry you now—not right this minute. It takes time to make all these arrangements, to work out details with Wykeham, to . . ."

"No problem there, Frankie. My father has already sent a letter to the earl, outlining some things your father agreed to years ago. I'm sure Wykeham will agree. Actually, I don't think he'd dare to disagree. He's still rather raw at this being an earl."

"What am I, a piece of property?" I cried. "Doesn't anyone care to consult me? It's my life that will be affected." I was angry and wasn't making very much sense, but I didn't care.

"Now, sweet," Harry said soothingly, coming around the chair to talk to me, much as one would talk to a whining child. "All brides get the jitters. There's nothing to be worried about. I'll take care of everything." He held me and kissed me while I tried desperately to keep my head from spinning. "Now, do you feel better?" he asked, smiling down at me.

I took a deep breath. "I'm not going to marry you immediately, Harry," I said stubbornly. "I need some time."

"Time!" Harry exploded, striding across the room and yelling at me. "Just what for? Do you think I have all the time in the world? And you—you're five and twenty. What makes you think you have time to waste?"

"There's no reason to be cruel, Harry," I said evenly, trying to hide the hurt.

"I'm only telling you the truth, Frankie." He looked at me, trying to master his anger. I hadn't seen him this way, ever. I thought I knew him better than I did. Finally, he seemed to overcome his rage, and he smiled at me. "I'm sorry, sweet," he said. "You don't know how very much I want you. That makes me want to get married immediately. My father seems to think we can have everything ready in a month. Will that be enough time for you?" He came across the room and took me in his arms. "Now, smile for me, sweetheart. Will a month give you enough time? Please say yes."

"Harry, please don't. I do need some time."

He smiled again and kissed me gently on each eye. "I understand that, my sweet. A month is a long time for me to wait for you. Remember that I've already waited for eight years to have you."

I decided not to mention the tales of the rice planter's daughter. "I can't say yes, Harry. I'll marry you, but I simply can't do it right away."

"There, see how easy that was? A month is a long time, and it's going to be even worse for me because I have some business in France and in the country, so I'll be away for part of the time. I'm going to miss you so much, Frankie."

He bent to kiss me again, but I dodged. "Harry, did you hear what I said?"

"Of course I did, sweetheart. You said you'd marry me." He managed to kiss me this time, and as usual, did a very expert and thorough job of it. I was completely breathless when he stopped. "I've got to run, my sweet. I'm going to the country tonight, but I should be back in a couple of days. If you want, we'll go shopping then, and I'll help you select some new gowns." He kissed me again, and then, with a flash of his smile, was out the door, leaving me staring at the place where he had been, not at all sure I had accomplished anything.

To my surprise, Wykeham arrived the next day. He was leaning rather heavily on his cane as Pinchbeck let him in, and was somewhat pale. I forced him to have some tea and go upstairs to rest before we talked. He complained, but he did not come down until the afternoon was almost over. I took advantage of the time to take a bath, put on a new dress, and have Katie do something with my hair. I'm not much of one for making an impression, and besides, Wykeham had seen me at my worst, but there was no reason to look dowdy.

When Wykeham came down for supper, he had also bathed and changed, and looked almost a new man. "I knew you needed to rest," I said, trying not to actually say "I told you so."

"Ever the nurse, aren't you?" he asked with a smile as we went in to eat. "Did you do all this?" he asked, indicating the draperies and silver. "Do you know you're amazing?"

I felt myself blush. "Sometimes," I admitted as he chuckled and held my chair for me. "Tell me," I said, as the new cook's efforts were brought in, "what brings you to London? And where is your sister?"

"Questions, questions," he said with a laugh, sampling the soup. "This is excellent. Your doing again?"

"Yes. You needed a decent cook. This one is French and rather expensive, I'm afraid, but I needed to get someone in a hurry, and he did have excellent references. I employed him on the spot."

Wykeham took another spoonful of soup. "I'm glad you did. My own cooking isn't nearly this tasty."

"*You* cook?" I felt myself staring at him.

He laughed at my expression. "Certainly. Out on the frontier, there aren't any cooks, French or otherwise. Of course, I could probably survive on hardtack and biscuits, but it does get old." He finished his soup. "As to your questions, in order—I came to London because I got a very curious letter from the earl of Mountnorris, and, two, Rebeckah is still at Foxcroft. I didn't want her to come up to London until the house was ready, and I wanted to see if you needed me to take care of anything. Besides, Rebeckah happens to be quite happy to remain at Foxcroft—David seems to have taken her under his wing."

I laughed. "David specializes in taking people under his wing."

"Especially those who have been hurt," the earl said, draining his wineglass. "I told him about Rebeckah's loss and he's been really amazing for her—takes her all about on walks and talks to her about the countryside. She's beginning to bloom again." The next course was brought in and Wykeham began to eat in silence.

"David's a wonderful companion," I said absently, wondering how to turn the conversation around to his first answer. There was no way, so I just asked. "Exactly what did Harry's father say to you in his letter?"

He looked at me over the top of his wineglass. "I wondered how long it would take you," he said with a grin. Then, to my exasperation, he began to eat again.

"Well?" I finally said, waiting.

"We really should wait until later to discuss this," he said. "That is, unless you prefer to talk about it now."

"Let's get it over with," I said grimly.

Wykeham laughed. "What a way to discuss your coming nuptials." He suddenly looked at me sharply. "Or do you feel that way? I thought you were looking forward to getting married, but I understood you planned to wait awhile. The earl of Mountnorris seemed to think you were in something of a rush." He paused a moment. "Are you?"

"No." I sounded bitter, so I tried to amend it. "That is, I

really think I need some more time. I feel the same way I did when we discussed this before.''

Wykeham nodded. ''I just wanted to see if you'd changed your mind. If you want more time, then you shall have it.'' He smiled at me. ''I'm wonderful at procrastinating when I have to.''

I was unbelievably relieved and smiled at him warmly. ''Thank you. I was afraid you wouldn't understand.''

''It's your mosaics, isn't it? This is really superb food.''

I shook my head. ''Not just the mosaics—it's the whole villa now, and the paper I want to write about it. That's very important to me. I don't really know why, but it's something I want to do before I give everything up.''

Wykeham looked at me in surprise. ''You don't have to give anything up, you know. And as for your paper, I understand about that perfectly. When it's read to such a stuffy group, it will rather validate everything you're doing.''

''They're not stuffy,'' I said. ''Yes, they are, and you're absolutely right.'' I felt tears behind my eyes. ''Thank you,'' I muttered again, trying hard not to cry in front of him. He was the only person in the world who understood how I felt.

''Hush that,'' he said with a smile, ''and eat something. My mother swears a good dinner will cure everything.'' He poured me some more wine and motioned for the next course. ''By the way,'' he dropped in casually, ''I don't want you to think the house and the letter were my sole reasons for coming here. I promised you I'd check on Babs, and I've begun some inquiries on that head.'' He looked at me and smiled smugly. ''Also, a rather odd thing happened. I received a visit from a very strange character—a chap named Peverell—who told me he was a Bow Street Runner and had information for me.''

''Oh!'' I gasped. ''I meant to tell you about that. I took it on myself to hire the Runners to investigate the theft and try to recover the stolen property. I never dreamed they would bother you with anything.''

''Good heavens, I wouldn't have it any other way. I would have done the same thing myself, except I probably would have tried to go investigate by myself, and gotten nowhere."

I was on pins and needles. "You are really the most maddening man. What did Peverell have to report?"

He smiled again and leaned back in his chair. He was obviously enjoying himself. "Well," he said slowly, "he told me that he has a very good lead. He seems to have discovered the general direction of the Skeltons. They must not be a very astute pair—according to Peverell, they seem to be leaving a trail of the stolen goods behind them. They're evidently selling things as they travel."

"Famous! This means it's only a question of time until they're caught, doesn't it?"

He leaned up against the table and frowned. "Probably, but from what Peverell tells me of the two, I suspect there may be more to it than a simple robbery by a pair of disgruntled servants."

"What do you mean?"

He shook his head. "Nothing, really. Just an idea of mine, you might say."

"What do you think? You really are the most exasperating man. I never know what you're thinking."

He laughed aloud. "That's as it should be," he said, his eyes crinkling at the corners. "I'll tell you right now what I'm thinking, though. I think we should go in and have a good game of chess, and then tomorrow you can show me around London. I'll play the rustic and we can see all the sights."

The next day was beautiful and sunny, and Wykeham, true to his word, went around to all the sights, wandering slowly to keep from tiring. It was a wonderful day, even though we were both exhausted by midafternoon. Being a tourist was harder than I had imagined. We ran into Lizzie in the afternoon, and asked about Babs.

"That girl," Lizzie said, making a face. "Now she's decided that she's going to be religious, and she's got Mademoiselle DeSalle taking her around to every church in London. Lord knows I can't think of anything more boring, but I suppose it's good for her soul."

"Are you talking about Babs or Mademoiselle DeSalle?"

I snapped. "Really, Lizzie, I can't imagine you letting them ramble about all alone. You know how Babs is. Besides, her last concern is her soul. She's into something, I know it."

"I trust Babs and Mademoiselle," Lizzie said stiffly. "After all, Frankie, you've been in the country so long that you don't realize how things are done here in London."

"I realize all too well," I shot back.

"Ladies," Wykeham said politely. "Perhaps we should discuss this later, over tea."

"There's nothing to discuss," Lizzie said, glaring at me.

"I'm sure you're right," Wykeham said, siding with Lizzie. I gave him a mean look, but he ignored it. "Perhaps we could talk to you later about this," he said politely to Lizzie. "As soon as the house is refurbished, we'll have a small dinner party. I want you to meet my sister, Rebeckah."

"Wonderful," Lizzie said. "I'll bring Babs along, well chaperoned." She stared at me pointedly before she rode away.

As soon as she was out of earshot, I turned on Wykeham. "Of all the silly, unthinking . . ." I ran out of words.

Wykeham put my arm through his and strolled along the edge of the park road. "You have such a turn with a phrase, Frankie," he said, quite effectively ignoring my outburst. "What's that building over there?"

"Go ask someone," I said nastily. I wasn't about to speak to him. The very idea of him standing up for Lizzie, when quite clearly the woman was not living up to her responsibility! I was angry.

Wykeham just laughed at me. "Not only a way with words, but such charm and finesse, as well. Remember that old adage about catching flies with honey? That's what I'm doing."

"With Lizzie or with me?" I snapped, glaring at him. I tried to walk away, but forgot he was holding onto my arm. I had to match my pace to his, and I could have sworn he deliberately slowed down. As it was, we ran right into Harry at the entrance to the park. Harry looked more surprised than I was.

"Wykeham," he gasped, before he collected himself. Then the color came back into his face. "How are you? Hadn't expected to see you in London today." Without waiting for an answer, he turned to me. "And how are you, Frankie?"

"I thought you were going to be out of town, Harry," I said, puzzled. "Wasn't that what you told me?"

A fleeting look I couldn't place passed over Harry's features. "I was slightly delayed, my dear. I'm leaving tomorrow, first thing. I was planning to come by and tell you."

"And where are you going?" Wykeham asked, displaying a shocking lack of manners.

"I have some business out of town," Harry said, neatly avoiding the question. I had to own that Harry did it well.

"Oh, really? What are you going to do?" Wykeham did it again.

Harry looked rather uncomfortable, and I didn't blame him. Wykeham knew better than to pry in such a manner. "Really," I said, "I'm sure Harry's business is quite personal. He'll probably tell us all about it when he returns."

"Quite right," Harry said. He turned to me. "Frankie, my dear, since I've seen you now and told you I'll be out of town, I won't come by tonight. I need to get up early and be gone. I'll be back as soon as possible." He looked at Wykeham. "Frankie and I have a great deal to discuss," he said with a smile.

Wykeham smiled back, but not with the same sort of smile. "True, and you and I also have a great deal to discuss."

Harry gave him a very strange look, and took his leave. I started to chastise Wykeham on his lack of manners, but he was staring after Harry with such a look that I stopped. I was trying to think of a way to find out what he was thinking when he took a deep breath and turned to me, almost as though he had put a mask on his face. "Shall we look at yet another monument, or do you prefer to go home?" he asked with a cheerful smile that never reached his eyes.

"I prefer to return home," I told him. He chattered on about the sights as we walked slowly back, but there was an underlying tension to him. I resolved to find out what was going on.

That night while we were again playing our after-dinner chess game, I tried every way I could think of to quiz him, but got nowhere. Finally, in desperation, I gave up all finesse.

"What on earth is bothering you?" I asked as he made a particularly bad move—one that he usually would not have made.

"Bothering me?" He looked up at me in feigned amazement. "Nothing at all is bothering me."

"Bosh," I said. "I may not be the most perceptive person in the world, but I pride myself on having a modicum of sense. Anyone who knows you at all would realize something is on your mind."

He gave me another smile that never reached his eyes. "Something besides chess?"

"Yes." I decided not to mince words. "Tell me what it is."

He looked at me thoughtfully. "Actually, I'm surprised you noticed. I thought I was covering rather well." He gave up and put a piece where I could check him. "If you don't mind, I'd rather not speak of it right now, but perhaps I can tell you later, when I have all the facts at hand."

"Is it something I can advise you about?" I asked, moving my piece. "Check."

He scarcely glanced down at the board. "No, not now." And that was all he would say. I prodded to no avail, but he did tell me he was returning to Foxcroft. "Don't you want to go back with me?" he asked, looking at me with those turquoise eyes. "You're almost finished here, and the weather's fine for working on your excavations."

"I need to stay and see to the upstairs rugs," I said.

"Fiddlesticks! How much expertise does it take to lay a rug?" he asked. "Pinchbeck and his wife can do that perfectly well."

I looked at him and smiled. "You've talked me into it," I said, "although it didn't take much effort on your part. I've itched to get back to my digging."

"Wonderful," he said, getting up and going over to the library desk. He removed a parcel from the drawer and brought it over to me. "I sent out for this today. I wanted to give you a present to show you how much I appreciated your hard work.''

"You didn't need to do that,'' I told him. I was quite overcome.

"I know I didn't need to,'' he said. "I wanted to.'' He handed me the parcel. "I hope you like it.''

I unwrapped the package and discovered a book. "I'm sure I will,'' I said, holding it.

"Look at the title,'' he prompted. "Then tell me if you like it.''

I turned the book over and looked at the engraving on the front. He had given me a beautifully bound copy of *Britannia*, by John Camden. I felt tears behind my eyes. "How did you know I wanted this?'' I asked around the lump in my throat.

"I guessed. Was I right?''

I nodded. "This is the guide for all English antiquaries. I've wanted a copy forever.'' I looked down and ran my hands over the book. "I can't thank you enough.'' I felt a tear spill over and run down my cheek.

He smiled at me. "You don't need to thank me at all. You've done more than enough for me already.'' He reached over and wiped the tear off my face with his fingertips. "None of that, now, or I'll be afraid to give you another gift.''

I caught my breath as he touched me. His touch was gentle and soft, and the smile he gave me brought out feelings I didn't know I had. "No other gift could ever be this wonderful,'' I stammered, trying to get back my equilibrium. My head was spinning.

"Don't tell me I must spend forever trying to top this,'' he said in mock horror. "At any rate, I hope you find it useful.''

"I shall.'' I looked down at the book and stared at it until the title came into focus.

"Could you plan to leave for Foxcroft tomorrow, or is that too soon?'' Wykeham asked cheerfully, evidently not seeing what kind of a state I was in.

"Certainly,'' I said, making an effort to breathe normally.

"I'd better go up right now and pack if we're to leave early."

"About noon, I thought, if that won't be inconvenient."

"Fine," I told him, clutching my book to my chest and fleeing. I ran up the stairs to my chamber, shut the door behind me, and leaned heavily against it. I was weak in the knees and breathing heavily. I really didn't know what was wrong with me. People had given me presents before, but nothing that meant so much to me as Camden's book.

I looked down at the book again and thought about the understanding that had prompted him to select this for me.

Whoever his Nancy was, I envied her.

Chapter 12

I was quite my old self by the time we left the next day. I suppose it was the thought of getting back to my digs. Katie rode with Wykeham and me in the carriage, and entertained us greatly by promptly going to sleep and snoring gently. Conversation was difficult with Katie's noise in the background. I probed Wykeham a little to try to discover what was bothering him, but he turned away all my efforts. I gave up eventually and got him to tell me all about life in the former colonies.

"It's quite wonderful," he sighed, finishing up a description of a trip he had made to a large river, the Mississippi.

"My goodness, I do believe you're still homesick!"

He gave me a sad smile. "I am. I'm going back someday, Frankie. Perhaps I'll have a son who will take over here, and I can go back and roam in the woods and mountains."

He sounded so wistful that I felt for him. "Perhaps," I agreed, just to be polite. I knew what it was like to wish dreadfully for something impossible. I changed the conversation to general remarks about the estate, and discovered he was already quite knowledgeable about the tenants, the rents, and, most especially, what needed to be done. We talked in that manner until we came to our inn.

Katie kept me awake most of the night complaining about her bed, and telling me that she needed her sleep, but couldn't shut her eyes. I pointed out that she had slept all day, but she denied it. As a result, I was fagged the next morning and showed it. Wykeham took one look at me and laughed aloud. "Those bloodshot eyes look like some I've seen after a long night in a tavern," he said between chuckles. "You are not, as they say, in face today."

"I fail to see the humor," I snapped.

To my chagrin, he only laughed at me and urged me to eat a good breakfast. "You can sleep all the way to Foxcroft," he said. "You and Katie can snore together."

"I don't snore," I said, glaring at him.

"Funny, I seem to remember that you do."

"It was your feverish imagination," I said, marching off toward the parlor.

When we were in the carriage, Katie promptly fell asleep again. "Now," Wykeham told me with a smile, "just close your eyes and I'll wake you up when we get to Foxcroft. And I won't even comment on your snoring."

"How many times do I have to tell you that I don't snore?" I snapped. "I have no intention of going to sleep." I turned away from him and closed my eyes for a moment to ease my aching head.

"Time to get up, sleepyhead," Wykeham said, shaking me not too gently. "We're at the Dower House."

I opened my eyes and stared blearily around me. We *were* home. I looked at him.

"Yes, you snore, but I did promise I wouldn't mention it. Do you want me to help you with your trunks?"

"I don't believe it for a moment, and no, you don't have to help me with my trunks. Griggins will see to them."

Wykeham shook Katie awake and helped both of us out of the carriage. It was only a little past noon, but I felt as weary as if it were midnight. Besides, my leg had gone to sleep, and I hobbled into the house trying to get the pins-and-needles feeling out of it. "Oh, my dear, is something wrong? Have you been hurt?" Clara cried, rushing to me and enveloping me in a cloud of powder and lavender. She was immediately joined by Charlie and the dog. Unfortunately, the dog, who was half grown now, leaped right up on me, knocking me back into Jervis, who fell right into Wykeham, who wound up in the dirt at the bottom of the step. We all rushed out to pick him up, but the dog got there first and lapped him quite noisily around the face.

"Lord, Frankie, get this infernal hound away from me," he gasped, knocking ineffectively with his hands. "This animal is worse than—" The dog sat down on his chest and kept him from saying anything else.

Clara and I pulled the dog off and gathered up Wykeham and his cane. "Come in and we'll dust you off," I offered.

He shook his head. "No, I think I'll go on to Foxcroft. If I stay here much longer, I'm going to be back in bed again. Perhaps you can come over tomorrow and meet Rebeckah."

I hadn't planned on doing anything except digging, but after we had ruined Wykeham's new coat, I couldn't refuse. "Of course," I told him as graciously as possible. "We'd all be delighted to meet your sister."

"We already know her," Charlie piped up. "We go walking with her and Dr. Watterson almost every day."

I stared at Charlie. "We?"

"I believe Miss Sophoronia is referring to herself and the dog," Clara said. "Although I usually go along, as well, and sometimes Annie walks with us." She looked from Wykeham to me, and evidently saw my surprise. "It's excellent exercise," she said nervously.

"I'm sure it is, Clara." I turned to Wykeham. "At any rate, we'll be over tomorrow."

As soon as the carriage drove off, I hurried inside and discovered that for all her vagueness, Clara had done a very creditable job with the house while I had been gone. When I commended her, she stammered and told me it was nothing. Actually, I was so overjoyed that I told her she could look after the house from now on, as I was going to be involved in my digging. I was very pleased with my inspiration to hire Clara. It was going to work out quite well.

The next day I had Griggins get everything ready, but left it to pay my duty call on Wykeham's sister. I told Griggins to be prepared to leave for the digs as soon as I returned. I planned to make this short. Charlie, Clara, and the dog went with me.

Brooks opened the door for us, and tried to shut it before the dog came in. From his manner, I suspected he had previous acquaintance with the animal. He, however, was unsuccessful. The dog bounded in and headed straight for the library door. Once there, he sat down in front of it and howled.

The door was jerked open and Wykeham stepped out. "Brooks! What the devil is . . ." That was as far as he got. The dog was on him, standing on its hind paws and licking Wykeham's face. "Frankie!" he roared, spotting me. "Come get this thing!"

Charlie and I dragged the dog off him and handed it over to Brooks, who promised to take it to the kitchen. "It seems, Wykeham, that you have acquired an admirer," I said, laughing. "That dog is quite attached to you."

"It's happened before," he said, going back into the library and easing into a chair. He seemed a little shaky, and I thought his fall the day before had been worse for him than he had indicated. "Dogs seem to develop a mad attachment for me." He squirmed in his chair to get comfortable and rang for some tea and cakes. "I'm sorry to tell you that Rebeckah isn't here right now. She went over to Pitchley to have tea with David's mother. She had been invited several days ago, and didn't want to break the engagement."

"I understand perfectly," I said, secretly glad that I could cut this short and get on back to my digging.

Wykeham smiled at Charlie. "I'm going to have to send for my dog so yours will have some company."

"Oh, famous!" Charlie squealed as she dashed over and perched on his lap. "Charlie!" I said. "Mind your manners!"

"Jeff doesn't mind," Charlie said. "He told me so. He said since I didn't have one, he'd be my father if I wanted."

"Jeff?" I almost choked at her easy familiarity with him. Then I stared at Wykeham. "You didn't have to do that."

"I know I didn't have to—I wanted to." He gave Charlie a hug. "Now, young lady, tell me what you've been doing with yourself while I've been gone. Have you been doing your lessons like you promised you would?'' He looked at Clara. "How about it, Miss Conroy? Has she been behaving herself?''

"Certainly,'' Clara said, beaming. I stared at the three of them. Evidently, they had become fast friends while I wasn't looking. When Brooks brought the tea in, Charlie slipped off Wykeham's lap and took her place beside Clara, as though she were quite accustomed to doing this. I started to make a comment, but just then we heard voices, and David came into the library, followed by one of the sweetest looking creatures I had ever seen. Even more amazing, they were holding hands.

David saw us, blushed furiously, then quickly drew himself up and allowed the woman to precede him into the library. "Ah, Rebeckah, there you are,'' Wykeham said. "Frankie, let me introduce you to my sister, Rebeckah.''

"Hello,'' I said rather absently. I was focusing my attention on David, trying to decipher his expression as he looked at her. I finally pinpointed it. "Good heavens!'' I said aloud.

They all looked at me quizzically, and I realized what I had said. "I was just amazed that you looked so much like your brother,'' I lied. I had to say something. I was in a state of shock. If David wasn't madly in love, I had never seen it. He kept staring at the girl, absolutely besotted. Of course, after I looked at her, I didn't blame him. She was of average height, with brown hair, the same turquoise eyes as Wykeham, and a creamy complexion. She had, however, the sweetest, most angelic expression I had ever seen. She certainly didn't mean to do it, but she had the effect of making me feel quite old and dowdy. I resolved to go back to the Dower House and have Katie do something different with my hair.

We stayed longer than I had planned, but the group was so congenial that we didn't notice. Wykeham was quite proud of his sister, and she was very concerned about him. David didn't do very much except sit and stare at Rebeckah, drinking in every word she uttered as though it were the gospels. I couldn't imagine David acting like this, but there he was, head over heels.

On the way back to the Dower House, I tried to get

information out of Clara, who was in transports over the romance. "Isn't it the most wonderful thing?" she gushed. "He fell in love with her the second he saw her."

"How do you know that?" I asked.

"I was there," she said in a theatrical whisper, "and I saw him look at her with love in his eyes."

"Now, really, Clara. He knew she'd been sick, and was probably looking at her quite professionally. He *is* a doctor, you know."

She shook her head. "No, it was love at first sight. It was so wonderful. I once read a novel just like that—the hero and heroine glanced at each other across a crowded room and knew they were bound to each other forever."

"Bosh," I said before I thought. I looked at Clara, and from her crestfallen expression thought she was going to cry, so I gave it up and changed the subject. It wouldn't hurt to let her have her illusions about love.

The next two weeks were heaven for me. The weather was quite fine and I spent my days digging and my nights writing. I knew I was going to have one of the best papers ever presented to the Society of Antiquaries. I wanted Wykeham to be proud of me when he presented it. I did take time to go over to Foxcroft several times to chat with him and Rebeckah. David was usually there.

"Aren't you neglecting your patients?" I asked him one day as we were leaving Foxcroft. He was still in somewhat of a daze.

"Not at all," he said. "After all, Wykeham's still weak enough to require that I check on him daily."

"And what about the days he was in London?" I asked dryly.

David had the grace to blush. "Well, of course, Frankie, I didn't want his sister to worry. After all, England is an unfamiliar land to her, and she has no friends here."

I laughed aloud. "Admit it, David. You've done the unthinkable—you're completely besotted."

"Don't be ridiculous!" He paused, but then gave in. "You're right," he admitted. "Frankie, it was so sudden that I couldn't believe it was happening. Isn't she the sweetest, most concerned, most caring creature you've ever seen?'' Actually, she was, but David didn't give me time to answer—he went on talking about Rebeckah. ''I tell you, Frankie, she's so wonderful, I can't believe she will even speak to me, much less think of caring about me. I'm afraid to say anything to her.''

''About the way you feel, you mean?''

He nodded. ''Yes. I wish I could, but I'm afraid she'll laugh at me, and I couldn't bear that. I do realize this is sudden, and we haven't known each other very long. Besides, she's suffered a tragedy.''

I nodded. ''I know. Wykeham told me.''

David stopped and looked at me in agony. ''Frankie, what if . . . what if she doesn't care for me at all? What if she's still in love with her dead fiancé?''

I reached out and put my hand on his arm. ''David, I don't think that's possible. Surely she's getting to know you in the same way that we do, and from what I've seen, I really believe she has the same feelings for you that you have for her.''

He stared at me, wanting so to believe me. ''Really, Frankie? Really? Do you think so?''

I tried hard not to chuckle at him. ''Truly, David. Clara even tells me it was love at first sight, and if there ever was an observer of romance, it's Clara. Why don't you talk to Rebeckah and tell her how you feel? She'll never know about your feelings if you don't declare yourself.''

''I don't know, Frankie. After what she's been through, I don't want to rush her.'' He paused, and a wistful look crossed his face. ''Although, Lord knows, I'd marry her tomorrow if I could.''

I looked at him and smiled. ''I know. David, I think she'd be glad to hear what you have to say. Rebeckah seems to have put the past behind her, and you're quite a wonderful person, you know. I really believe she would welcome an offer from you.''

''Do you really think so?'' he asked. I started to say yes, but didn't have the chance. David grabbed my arms and hugged me. ''Frankie, you're priceless. I'll do it!'' With that, he gave me a quick kiss on the forehead. ''I'll love you forever for this,'' he said as he went off toward Pitchley, whistling under his breath. I went on to the Dower House in a very fine frame of mind, feeling like a very capable matchmaker. Everything seemed to be going well.

Harry came to the Dower House to see me that night.

I was working on my paper for the Society of Antiquaries when Jervis announced that Harry was waiting to see me. I glanced at the clock and saw it was almost eleven. I looked at Jervis, startled that Harry would come unannounced and so late.

"Shall I tell him you are not available?" Jervis asked frigidly. He obviously didn't approve.

I shook my head and hid my papers. "No, Jervis, show him in. It may be an emergency."

Jervis bowed stiffly and ushered Harry into the library, pulling the door almost closed, but not quite. I walked over and shut it firmly.

"Just what is this all about, Harry?" I asked, remembering the last time he had come by so late. I was determined to keep things on an even keel this time. I went back and sat down behind the desk, to keep its bulk between us.

Harry lounged in a chair in front of the desk and stretched his legs out in front of him. His boots were very dusty, and his clothes looked as though he had been riding hard. "Just came by to see my bride-to-be," he said with a smile.

I smiled back—I couldn't help myself. "What else, Harry?"

"Dash it all, Frankie, do you always have to think I have a reason for coming to see you? Can't you just think I've been dying of love for you or some such thing?"

I shook my head. "Hardly, Harry."

There was a short silence between us as Harry helped himself to a glass of whiskey from the table and sipped it. "Did you get the London house ready?" he asked casually.

I nodded. "It was a job replacing everything that was taken, but I think it's better than it was before. Except the silver, of course. I couldn't replace what had been taken."

"It must have been a terrible experience for you, coming in and finding things missing," he said, staring at me intently as he sipped another glass of whiskey. I couldn't fathom his expression.

"Yes," I agreed, "but I did set the Bow Street Runners out after the Skeltons, so I hope to recover something. I think a runner has recently been to see Wykeham with some discoveries."

Harry sat up quickly. "Really," he said casually, belying his posture. "What have they discovered?"

I shrugged. "I really don't know. Wykeham is handling it." I changed the subject. "Have you finished your business in the country? I thought you might be headed back to London." I glanced at his dusty clothing.

"I've been in London," he said, "and I came here expressly to talk to you, Frankie. We've got to get things settled between us."

I refused to meet his eyes. "What do you mean, Harry?"

"You know very well what I mean, Frankie." He set his glass down hard on the table and his tone was grim. My father told me that Wykeham said it would take several weeks to make all the arrangements. You and I know that isn't so. Why the delay?"

"It just takes time, Harry," I said evasively.

He leaned toward the desk and spoke sharply. "Don't lie to me, Frankie. Why the delay? You don't have to put up with Wykeham's dawdling. You're of age, you know."

I forced myself to meet his eyes. "I needed some time, Harry."

"For what?" He sounded petulant. "I told you I didn't want to wait, and I still see no reason to."

"I need time to finish my digging and write a paper." There, it was out. I took a deep breath, waiting for the explosion. There was a pause before Harry realized what I had said.

"*Your digging*! My God, Frankie, you'd put that piddling in the dirt ahead of me!" He stood and came around the desk to stand over me. "I had no idea you were so stupid."

It was my turn to leap up. "Stupid! Don't you dare say that to me! Not ever, Harry."

"It *is* stupid," Harry said. "How you could ever consider something that ridiculous as important is quite beyond me."

He seized me by the shoulders. "Dammit, Frankie, I can't believe you're doing this to me."

"It will only be a few weeks, Harry," I said, taken aback by his violent response.

Harry turned away from me and walked over to the fireplace, running his hands through his hair. "I can't wait, Frankie, not even a few weeks. I won't, do you hear me? We'll get married right away or not at all—is that clear?"

I felt myself go rigid. "Is that an ultimatum, Harry?" I asked quietly, suddenly as cold as ice all over.

"You can consider it that if you want to." He turned and looked at me. "I call it a practical response. You're putting me off for no reason at all except your own selfish whims."

"My excavation is important to me, Harry," I said. "I wish you'd see that."

Harry made an effort to control himself. After a moment, he looked at me and smiled, but it never reached his eyes. He came over to me and put his arms around me. "I'm sorry," he said. "This is no way for us to discuss this."

I moved back, putting the desk chair between us. "Don't do that, Harry. Every time you want something, you think all you have to do is hug me and smile, and I'll give in. It won't work this time—we need to sort this out."

A hard look came over his face, and he moved away. "All right," he said shortly, "but I really don't think there's much to discuss. You had a choice to make, and evidently you've made it."

"My choice was to marry you," I reminded him, "and if you loved me, you'd give me time. You'd be glad that I was doing this."

"Glad! Glad!" He moved back to the fireplace. "You really think I should be glad that I'll be the laughingstock of London when everyone in the *ton* finds out that you prefer digging in the dirt for a piece of pottery to marrying me."

"That isn't true, Harry."

He came up close to me. "No? Well that's the way it looks to me, and I think everyone else will see it that way, as well."

I wanted to deny it, but I knew the *ton* well enough to know he was right. "All right, Harry," I heard myself say.

"I'll marry you, but please give me two weeks. That isn't very long."

"It's a long time for me," he said. He put his fingers under my chin and turned my face up so he could look into my eyes. "Are you putting me off for another reason?"

I blinked. "No. What other reason could there possibly be?"

"Wykeham."

"Wykeham?" I said blankly. "Whatever would he have to do with anything? He's promised to present my paper, but what else could there be?"

Harry collapsed back into the chair in front of the desk and looked steadily at me. "I thought you might be in love with him."

It was my turn to stare. "You thought I was in love with him? Are you mad, Harry?"

"Just practical," he said, with another smile. "I've seen it happen before when two people are in proximity."

"Well, it hasn't happened this time, and it won't," I told him, sitting down behind the desk. I was quite wobbly.

Harry regarded me for a few moments as he finished his whiskey, and I tried my best to meet his gaze, but my eyes fell and I felt an unexpected blush on my cheeks.

"Do you have any money in the house?" Harry asked.

I looked up, startled. "What?" I wasn't sure I had heard him correctly.

"Do you have any money in the house?" he repeated. "I hate to ask, but if we're going to be married, I suppose it's all right." He smiled again, but his eyes were cold. "I'm a little under the hatches right now and need a little quick blunt. After we're married, it won't make any difference—it'll all be coming out of the same pocket."

I wanted to ask whose pocket, but held my tongue. "What about an advance from your father?" I asked after a short pause. "Have you applied to him?"

Harry gave a short, bitter laugh. "I might as well apply to the devil for all the good my father does me. I told you before that he controls the purse strings and likes to see me writhe and beg." His face twisted. "I vowed I wouldn't do that again."

I was shaken by his bitterness. "I can't help you, Harry. I don't keep anything here except enough for the barest household expenses. I could ask Wykeham, though."

"No!" The word exploded in the room. "I refuse to be considered a charity case."

"I'm sorry, Harry—it was a thoughtless remark on my part." I looked at him and felt pity for him. He did look defeated. "Let me give you what I have. It isn't very much, but perhaps it will help."

There was no sound in the room except the crackle of the fire on the grate as I got the strongbox from the bottom drawer and cleaned it out. There truly wasn't very much, as I had paid the household bills the week before. I put the notes in an envelope and handed it to Harry.

"This is only a loan until we get married," he said, putting it inside his coat.

"That's understood," I said.

He gave me a flash of his old smile and leaned over and kissed me lightly on the forehead. "Two weeks," he said, almost jovially.

"Two weeks," I promised.

He moved to the door. "I must go, my sweet. I had no wish to impose on either Wykeham or Watterson, so I've bespoke a room at the inn. I won't be back tomorrow because I need to leave for London at first light. I'll expect you in London in a week and a half or so?"

I nodded. "I'll be there."

He blew me a kiss and started out the door. "Till then, my little love." With that, he was out the door and gone.

I leaned back in my chair and put my hands over my eyes. The scene seemed almost like a dream—a nightmare, rather. What was wrong with Harry? I thought for the better part of an hour and never reached a conclusion. Several things bothered me about what he had said. It also bothered me that he had borrowed money, although what was wrong with it escaped me. It simply didn't seem right. I knew Harry's father was strict, but he had always been accounted fair. This treatment of Harry didn't match what I had always heard of the man.

One other thing upset me considerably: why had Harry

asked if I was in love with Wykeham? It was true that the more I knew of him, the more I respected and admired him, but *love*? I was in love with Harry. Every time he kissed me, I felt giddy. Wasn't that what love was?

I sat and thought until the fire died down and the room began to have a touch of the night chill in it. I hadn't reached any conclusions. The only thing I had done was to confuse myself thoroughly—and give myself a splitting headache.

For the first time in a long while, I didn't think about my mosaics when I went to bed. I thought about Harry until I had exhausted every possible avenue. I didn't know what to do or how to interpret his behavior. I tried to force myself to think about my villa and compose lines of my paper. It didn't work, but at least I wasn't thinking about Harry anymore.

The last image in my mind before I finally went to sleep was Wykeham's. He was well and healthy, but was dancing with a beautiful lady in a blue dress. I distinctly heard him call her Nancy.

It was a restless night.

Chapter 13

When I arose the next day, I had to force myself to get out and go to my digs. Once there, I was fine, and worked steadily through nuncheon. If I were going to complete things in a fortnight, I would have to work doubly hard during the day and devote my evenings to my notes and my paper. I was determined to finish as much as I could.

"You're looking like a fishwife today, Frankie." The comment was accompanied by a laugh.

I jumped to my knees, spilling dirt all over me. It wasn't noticeable, as I was already covered with dirt from top to bottom. I glanced down at my clothing. "I deny that, David. No fishwife ever got this dirty."

He laughed and held out a hand to me. "Come out of the dirt and talk to me a moment." He held me while I jumped a trench and we stood at the edge of the field. "How's it going?"

"Famous! I've uncovered what I think is the atrium of a villa, and I'm getting some wonderful notes on it." I glanced at him. "Did I tell you that Wykeham is going to present a paper for me to the Society of Antiquaries?"

David glanced down at me. "How did you coerce him into that?"

"Coerce! David, you should know me better than that. I'll have you know he *offered* to do it. Of course, if he hadn't, I'm sure I would have found a way. But truly, he did offer on his own."

"What Wykeham goes through for you. I'm amazed."

"Well, not every man of my acquaintance is a gentleman like he is," I said pointedly. "Most prefer to concentrate on my faults."

"I wouldn't dare," David said in mock horror. "I spend all my time telling everyone what a paragon you are." I had no reply for this obvious falsehood, except to make a face at him. "Seriously, Frankie," he said, "I came by to tell you I'm on my way."

"On your way where?" I asked blankly.

David looked impatient with me. "Frankie, don't you remember our conversation yesterday? I'm on my way to Foxcroft to talk to Rebeckah. I'm going to tell her how I feel, and if she seems to reciprocate my feelings, I'm going to offer for her." He paused and stared at me. "Yesterday, you thought I should. Don't you think so now?"

"Oh, yes, by all means. I think it's definitely what you should do."

David seemed relieved. "Good. Are you *sure* I should?"

I gave him a small push. "Go, David. And don't come back until you talk to her. Be sure to let me know what she says."

"What if she refuses? What if she laughs?"

"She won't. Now, go." I gave him another push and saw

him off down the edge of the field. He was the worst mix of uncertainty I had ever seen. Wykeham wouldn't act that way, I was sure.

Griggins and I worked until well into the afternoon, and by then, I was exhausted. As soon as I got back to the Dower House, I ordered a bath and a change of clothes. Katie was duly horrified at my appearance. "It ain't right, you mucking around in the dirt," she muttered.

"I *like* mucking around in the dirt, Katie, and I don't care whether it's right or not. I'm discovering all sorts of new things."

"You'll catch a disease, that's what. Now, you get into the tub and scrub. I'll lay out some decent clothes."

I gave up—Katie was incorrigible, but the bath was heavenly. I soaked until the water got tepid, then got out and put on clean clothes—a sprigged muslin Katie and I had recently made over. It looked very fine, if I said so myself. The green ribbons set it off nicely and went well with my skin and eyes. Katie wanted to put a ribbon in my hair, but by the time she had brushed out all the tangles, I settled for something simple. One more stroke with that hairbrush and I was convinced I would have a headache for life.

It was a while before supper, but almost time for tea, so I decided to go to Foxcroft and have it with Wykeham. I was curious about David and Rebeckah, since he hadn't come by with any news. I would have hated to have given him the wrong advice.

Wykeham was propped up on the sofa in the library, one leg negligently stretched out on the sofa, one resting on the carpet. At first I thought he was sleeping, but on closer look, I realized he was staring out the open library window. "Being homesick again?" I asked briskly.

He jumped and looked guilty. "No. Well, maybe a little," he admitted. "Actually, I was waiting for David and Rebeckah to come back."

I sat and rang for some tea, as I usually did. "Come back from where? Good heavens!" I sat up straight as a thought hit me. "David hasn't talked her into eloping to Gretna, has he?"

Wykeham laughed. "I certainly hope not. I believe in long engagements, myself."

I wanted to ask him about Nancy, but I held my tongue. "You knew David was going to offer for Rebeckah, then?"

"He told me, and I gave him my blessing, for what it's worth. I also warned him that Rebeckah, for all her fragile appearance, is as hard as nails. The man will have to spend his life doing whatever she wants."

I grinned at him. "Poor David is so besotted that I'm sure he plans to do just that."

Wykeham grinned as Brooks brought in the tea. I poured him a cup. He leaned back against the back of the sofa and looked at me. "I enjoy these afternoons immensely, do you know that?"

"I should hope so, as I enjoy them myself. It's my contribution to your well-being." I grinned at him. "I shall hate to lose this when you and Rebeckah go to London."

"You could go along." He looked at me over the rim of his cup.

"I'll probably already be there." I paused, wondering how to broach the subject of Harry. There was only one way, I decided. "Harry came to visit me last night," I said.

To my surprise, he didn't seem shocked. "I heard he was in the neighborhood," he said. "I thought perhaps he might drop by the Dower House." He handed me his cup for a refill. "I hope you know I'm going to change to drinking coffee in this house. I really can't abide this stuff. I make Brooks pour out the tea when you're not here. I'm even turning Mrs. Simms into a coffee drinker."

"Stop changing the subject," I told him. "Who told you Harry was around?"

"Just a friend," he said with a shrug. I immediately suspected David.

"Wykeham, I'm not sure I believe you," I said.

"Do you know you're the only person who calls me Wykeham? I distinctly remember asking you to call me Jeff."

"I prefer Wykeham," I said with a smile. "It gives you a little dignity."

He threw back his head and laughed. "Touché. I asked

for that, didn't I? Well, let me tell you this: I've decided I *like* for you to call me Wykeham.''

''You might as well'' I told him, ''because that's what I intend to call you. It suits you.'' I put my cup down on the table. ''Now, tell me what you heard about Harry.''

He looked at me innocently. ''Not a thing, really. Just that he was in the neighborhood. What did he want, by the way?''

''He wanted me to agree to marry him right away,'' I said, leaning against the back of my chair. I couldn't look straight at Wykeham. Briefly, I recounted Harry's visit, omitting the request for money.

''So, you have a fortnight to finish everything,'' he said when I had finished. ''Is that what you want—to get married then?''

I took a deep breath. ''Yes.'' I wasn't sure if it was the truth or not, but I was committed. ''I promised Harry I'd come up to London and we'd be married.''

''If it's what you want to do, I won't stand in your way at all,'' he said carefully. ''I'll write the earl of Mountnorris right away and tell him there's no reason to delay any longer. There is one thing though, Frankie,'' he began, then paused.

''And that is?'' I prompted.

''I want to make arrangements for your jointure to stay in your own name, if possible. I want you to have access to it, rather than turn the whole thing over to Harry.''

I had never considered this. ''Can that be done?''

''In point of fact, no. Not directly, but there are ways around it. I checked with a solicitor.'' He glanced at me to gauge my reaction. ''Is that agreeable with you?''

I nodded. ''Fine.''

There was a small, awkward silence between us. Finally, he asked me to stay for supper, but I declined. Then he asked if I would come by for supper the next night. ''If we're fortunate,'' he said with a laugh, ''Rebeckah and David will join us to announce their engagement.''

''Don't count your chickens too early,'' I reminded him.

''I don't think we have to worry about those two particular chickens,'' he said with a smile. ''Will you be here?''

"You couldn't keep me away," I told him as I went out the door.

The next evening, Clara and Charlie set up a howl when I told them I was going to Wykeham's for supper and that David and Rebeckah might have an announcement. "Oh, how I would love to be there," Clara said, clasping her hands to her skinny bosom and rolling her eyes heavenward. "Will you remember to tell us all about it—every single word?"

"I'll remember, I promise," I said as I not too gently removed Charlie's dog from my chest. He was trying to wash my face for me. "Charlie, if you don't get this animal outside, I'm never going to let you go anywhere again. Ever."

Charlie made a futile effort to make the dog stay down, and it took the three of us—Charlie, Clara, and myself—to get the creature outside. "That dog is going to have to learn some manners, or it's going to find another home," I threatened.

"He can live over at Foxcroft," Charlie said. "Jeff already has a dog and I know he'd like to have another one."

"Nonsense," I said. "The man has troubles enough without that horrid dog crawling all over him and the furniture. I expect you to make it a bed in the stables and keep it there. Besides," I gave her a glare that was ineffective, "I want you to stop calling him Jeff. You are to address him properly."

Charlie gave me a stubborn look that I knew meant she didn't intend to change her ways, but I didn't have time to argue. I was on my way out the door and off to Foxcroft. David hadn't been by, and to tell the truth, I was as curious as Clara.

Brooks ushered me into the parlor, where I expected to see Wykeham, David, and Rebeckah, but only Rebeckah was there to greet me. She was radiant.

"Do come in," she said warmly, holding out her hands. "I'm sorry Jeff isn't here to greet you, but he and David are in the library with a caller."

I was immediately consumed with curiosity. "A caller?" I asked casually. "Anyone I might know?"

Rebeckah shook her head as she led me to the small parlor. "Oh, no, I'm sure you don't know this person. He seems to be a thoroughly disagreeable sort."

"Rather like Perkins?" I asked dryly.

She laughed—a deep chuckle that reminded me of her brother. "This character makes Perkins look unbelievably respectable. Sit and we'll talk until David and Jeff get here."

"Do I get to hear good news, or must I wait until everyone gets here?" I asked with a smile.

She blushed rosily. "You've guessed, then."

I couldn't restrain my laughter. "Absolutely. Although I told your brother not to count his chickens."

"He wants us to wait for a while—at least until Mother can get here, or else we should plan to go to Virginia for the wedding." She leaned toward me. "I was so surprised that this should happen. David is such a wonderful person."

"That he is, and I think he's doing quite well for himself," I said matter-of-factly. "I'm sure the two of you will rub along quite well together." There was a small silence, and I found myself chattering to fill the space. "Weddings seem to be in the air just now. I'm planning to be married shortly myself."

Rebeckah looked up at me in surprise. "Married! But I had so hoped . . ." She stopped and began again. "That's wonderful. Is he anyone I've met?"

"Harry Apsley," I said shortly. "I'm not sure you've met him. He's been in the neighborhood, but I don't think he's been at Foxcroft."

We were interrupted by a noise in the hall. I jumped up and ran to the door and opened it a crack, trying in vain to see exactly which thoroughly disreputable character was visiting Wykeham now. The man was out the door before I could get a good look at him, and I had to hurry to my chair before David and Wykeham barged into the parlor. Rebeckah was going into whoops of laughter as I tried to compose myself, and the two men looked from one of us to the other. "Just what is going on here?" Wykeham demanded.

Rebeckah mopped at her eyes. "Not a thing, dear brother."

He looked at me. "All right, Frankie, confess."

"Why would you think I would . . ." I began.

"Because I know you. Now, confess."

I gave up. "There's nothing to confess. I was merely trying to get to the door in time to discover exactly who was being whisked in and out so we couldn't discover his identity."

"Why didn't you simply ask me?" Wykeham said, as David went over to sit beside Rebeckah. "We were having a visit from Peverell."

"Peverell?" I searched my memory. "The Bow Street Runner! Did he have news? What did he say? Have you discovered anything about the silver?"

Wykeham groaned and held up a hand. "No more, please. One question at a time. Yes, Peverell had some news, but I can't divulge it right now. And yes, he thinks he may be on the track of the silver." He held out a hand for me. "Now, let's go eat and talk about some good news. Has Rebeckah told you?"

I nodded and looked at Rebeckah and David. "I told you so, David," I said, unable to resist.

Supper was an animated affair, and by the time we went to the library for a game of cards afterward, it was as though we had all been friends for years.

"Frankie's getting married soon," Rebeckah told David as we sat around the table, not playing cards, but talking and drinking coffee.

David looked at me sharply. "To Harry?"

I nodded. I didn't really want to talk about it in front of Wykeham and David. "I have some things to do first," I said, "and then I need to make sure the girls are going to be taken care of—especially Babs." I looked at Wykeham. "I know you'll be responsible for them, but I still feel that I need to look after them." There was a short, awkward pause. "And, of course, I'm sure Harry will feel the same way. After all, he knows we're all still a family."

"I'm sure he will," Wykeham said, rather stiffly I thought. "Still, they're primarily my responsibility."

"I haven't met all of them, have I?" Rebeckah asked. "I do know Charlie, Annie, and Clara, of course."

"Sophoronia," I corrected. "That's Charlie's real name, and I can readily understand why she renamed herself. I only wish she had resorted to Mary or Sally, or even Phoebe. Charlie just isn't very suitable."

Wykeham chuckled. "I don't know about that—it seems to suit Charlie just fine. I couldn't think of a better name for her."

"I think she'll grow out of it," I said. "Perhaps when she goes to London for her coming out. I doubt if she'll wish to be introduced as Miss Charlie Martin."

"I think it has a ring to it," Wykeham said. "Have you heard from Babs?"

"Babs?" Rebeckah asked, looking at me.

"One of my other sisters," I explained. "She's in London being looked after by my sister, Lizzie. Or rather, I hope she's looking after her—Babs has a tendency toward the melodramatic, as well as being the most scatterbrained chit alive."

"I'm sure she's fine," David said, stifling a yawn. "I'm going to have to go home."

I took that as a hint and, since he offered to drive me, left with him. I had another motive, as well. As soon as we were in the carriage, I started on him. "Tell me, David, exactly what did Peverell say to Wykeham? You know you can confide in me."

"I'd as soon confide in the *Times*," David said, pausing in his laughter. "Did you think to cozen me into telling you something?"

"Well, yes." I tried another tack. "You know how distressed I was when I discovered the theft. Wouldn't you like to let me know how the investigation is going?"

"It's going just fine," David said, "and I think Peverell will have it solved very shortly. He's quite good at what he does."

"What is he doing?" I slipped the question in as innocently as I could. Unfortunately, we stopped at the door of the Dower House just then, and David used that as an excuse not to answer.

"You'll find out all too soon, Frankie," he said, "and I want you to know that you can depend on me as a friend."

"What does that mean, David?"

He helped me down from the carriage. "I can't say more. Just remember that. I'm sure Wykeham feels the same way. Good night."

With that, he was off, leaving me standing on my doorstep, thoroughly puzzled.

———— Chapter 14 ————

The next week passed in a frenzy of work—letters to London to inform Jane, Lizzie, and Babs of my forthcoming marriage, and nights spent working until the late hours on my paper. The paper was rapidly taking shape, and I thought it would make quite a stir when Wykeham presented it. The mosaics I had found were remarkably complete, and I thought further excavations might yield even more. I didn't even want to think about any more excavations, for whenever I did, I felt like crying. I wished a thousand times that Harry were as understanding as Wykeham. But Harry was Harry, and I was betrothed to him. That meant no more excavations after this one. I worked from early morning until late in the afternoon like a person possessed. I was determined to finish as much as possible.

Rebeckah stopped by one Tuesday afternoon. There had been a light drizzle in the morning, and the field was still muddy. I hadn't wanted to work, but dared not stop. I had only a few days until I had to leave for London. I was on my knees, raking through the mud, when I heard Rebeckah call my name.

"Hello, Frankie! I don't mean to bother you, but I thought I'd stop and say hello."

I got up from the mat I had been kneeling on and knocked as much mud as possible from my skirt. "You would never bother me," I told her, hopping over a trench and skirting around the edge of the field. "I'm delighted to see you."

"I'm lonesome at Foxcroft since Jeff left, and thought I'd go for a walk. This is a beautiful place."

I skipped the amenities. "Your brother's gone? Where to? Has he heard something from the Runners about the robbery?"

Rebeckah laughed. "Jeff was right about your questions. Yes, he went up to London for a day or two. He said he'd be right back, though. As for the Runners, I'm afraid I don't know anything."

I laughed along with her. "I have a tendency to get carried away," I said. "Even with this." I gestured toward my digs. "I've been spending every minute here."

"What are you doing?" She glanced around with curiosity.

I explained in detail about my mosaics and about the paper I was writing. I had expected the usual reaction, but, to my delight, she responded in the same way her brother had. "That's wonderful," she said. "I think you must lead a very interesting life, Frankie."

"Interesting?" I had never thought of my life as interesting at all. "I'm afraid not. This fascinates me, but it's a great deal of hard work." I glanced around. "At any rate, it's almost over. After tomorrow I must stop and get ready to go up to London."

"Oh, yes. You're to be married," she said. "I rather envy you that, as well. Jeff insists that David and I must wait until Mother gets here. Of course, I do want her here."

"You've invited your mother to come to Foxcroft?"

Rebeckah looked at me and laughed. "I haven't seen you since the latest developments, have I? Evidently, I'm not alone in worrying about my incorrigible brother. Jeff was about to write Mother and tell her about my engagement, when we received a letter from her that she was preparing to leave Virginia and join us. When I left, she said she wanted to come with me, but couldn't leave. It seems she changed her mind." Rebeckah laughed. "She's on her way now."

"I'm delighted for you," I said. "That means you and David won't have to wait so long."

"I'm glad your plans are working out, as well, Frankie," she said. "I had hoped . . . I thought that perhaps . . ." She stopped and began again, on another subject, it seemed to me. "I'll hate to see you settle in London. I had hoped we would be close friends." She looked at me and smiled. "But I'm sure I shall be delighted to meet your Harry and we can all be friends."

"Yes." I didn't know what else to say. It hadn't really come home to me that I would be living somewhere else. I had thought about it briefly, but I always thought of myself as being at the Dower House. "I'm sure Harry will want to entertain when we're in London. You'll like him." I smiled at her. "Everyone does."

"Splendid. I'm anxious to meet him. Jeff hasn't told me very much about him. By the way, are Jeff and I invited to the wedding?"

My eyes widened. "Of course. Harry was going to get a special license, so it will be very small, just the families, but you're now part of the family. I certainly want you to be there."

"Famous," she said with a laugh. "I had hoped so. Jeff has promised to take me up to London next week, so we'll already be there. The city will be quite a treat for me, and I think even Jeff is looking forward to it."

"Wonderful," I said hollowly.

"I want to tell you now, while we have the time," Rebeckah went on, "that I appreciate everything you've done for Jeff. You've made him feel welcome here."

"Welcome!" I almost choked. "Did he tell you how he was hurt?"

Rebeckah's eyes met mine. "Yes, and neither of us blames you at all. You more than made up for what happened by taking care of Jeff the way you did."

"He's a wonderful person," I said, meaning it. "Sometimes I almost envy Nancy."

"Nancy?" Rebeckah sounded blank.

I stared at her. "Yes, Nancy. He kept saying her name in his delirium. He must care for her very much." I paused while I searched for words. "He told me as much one time."

"Nancy, my goodness. Oh, he does care about her!" Rebeckah said.

I felt my heart sink right into my muddy shoes. "I thought so," I managed to say.

"As a matter of fact," Rebeckah said, "Nancy is coming over with Mother. Jeff is certainly looking forward to seeing her."

"I imagine he is," I said. My lips felt wooden. I had known all along that there was someone named Nancy, but Rebeckah's confirmation seemed to put up a door. Now there would be someone else drinking tea or coffee and playing chess with Wykeham—someone named Nancy.

After Rebeckah left, the drizzle began again, then changed to rain, mirroring my disposition. In disgust, I hastily covered up my trenches as best as I could, and Griggins and I went back to the Dower House. I was in a foul mood.

I forced myself to work on my paper. I had the first draft ready, and was trying to revise. After a dozen attempts to rework my sentences, I wound up spilling ink over my foolscap notes. In disgust, I threw the whole thing in a drawer and slammed it shut. Clara was sitting on the sofa, doing her embroidery and keeping me company. "Oh, dear," she said as I crashed the drawer into the desk. "Is your work not going well?"

"No," I snapped. "Not at all, and I must finish it so I can go up to London."

There was a long silence, punctuated only by the hissing of a very small fire on the grate. Finally, Clara spoke. "Do you really think it's wise, Frankie?"

"What? Finishing my paper? I have to do it. Wykeham has promised to deliver it for me, and I want it to be the best I can possibly do."

Clara looked visibly agitated, and stuck herself with her needle. She started to speak, but had to wait while she sucked on her injured finger. Then she looked at me and spoke, all in a rush. "I don't mean the paper, dear. I was thinking that perhaps this hurry to get married wasn't, ah, all the thing. Perhaps your feelings for Harry. . . . Perhaps you should reconsider and, ah, think and, ah, um. . . ."

I sat down beside her. "Please don't worry, Clara. I know Wykeham plans to keep you on as a companion for Charlie and Annie. The three of you will most likely come live with

Harry and me. I couldn't get on without you." I glanced down at the furry mass at my feet. "Although I would love to leave this animal behind. Do you think Wykeham would take him?"

"I'm sure of it. He's very fond of dogs and children, you know."

I looked at her in surprise. "No, I didn't know, although I do recollect he once told me he owned a dog."

Clara nodded and tried again. "It wasn't my position I was worried about, Frankie. I know you might feel it isn't my place to say this, but . . ." She stopped.

Clara's maddening habit of never ending her sentences irritated me, but I was determined to be patient. "Yes, Clara?"

"I don't think you should get married," she blurted out all at once. "At least, not to Harry Apsley. You don't love him." She ended on a wail.

I patted her hand. "Of course I love Harry, Clara. I assure you that I've thought this through very carefully."

She shook her head. "No, you don't love him at all," she said firmly. "I know all the signs."

I laughed aloud. "Are you worried because Harry and I don't behave like Rebeckah and David? If that's what's bothering you, Clara, I can assure you that Harry and I have known each other so long that such behavior is not necessary."

"You're *acquainted* with him, but I don't think you *know* him," Clara said. "Oh, dear, I've said the wrong thing." She looked at me with tears in her eyes. "I do apologize."

"You don't need to apologize, Clara. I appreciate your concern."

"Then, you'll reconsider? I know if you but took the time to think about Lord Harry, you'd realize that you really care for . . ."

"That I really care for Harry," I finished for her. "I'm sure I would, Clara."

"That wasn't what I meant," Clara said stubbornly.

"Then what, Clara?"

"Wykeham," she blurted out. "You care for him."

I was thoroughly confused. "Wykeham? What are you talking about, Clara? Of course I care for Wykeham. He's one of my dearest friends. I don't know what I would have done without his support for my work.''

''That's what I mean,'' Clara said, beginning to cry again. ''Oh, dear, I've simply made things worse.'' She jumped up and rushed out of the room, leaving her embroidery on the sofa, and leaving me thoroughly confused. After picking up her embroidery and discovering another book printed by Minerva Press hidden underneath it, I finally concluded that Clara had been reading too many romantic novels again.

It rained again the next day, and again I tried in vain to work on my paper. Eventually, I gave that up and dragooned Clara into helping me sort through my wardrobe. There wasn't time for new dresses, and I needed to find something to use for my wedding. After much debate, we decided there was nothing suitable, and I was forced to write Lizzie and ask her to look through her dresses and select something. I didn't particularly like the idea of getting married in a borrowed dress, but supposed it was better than saying my vows while dressed in my best—a black bombazine I had made for Papa's funeral.

I also spent a goodly amount of time trying to talk to Clara, but she was as close as a clam. No matter what tack I took, she refused to say anything except to tell me she had already said more than she should have. It was altogether a most dismal day. The high point was after supper, when we were all sitting around the library telling stories. Charlie's dog suddenly started baying and ran to the front door. The moment Jervis pushed the animal aside long enough to open the door, it bounded out and right on top of someone. As we all rushed to the door, I had to put my hands over Charlie's ears. There was the distinct sound of a man cursing very fluently.

Moving Jervis aside and handing Charlie to Clara, I peered around the door. There was poor Wykeham on the steps again, his face being thoroughly washed by the dog. ''For God's sake, Jervis, will you get this animal off me,'' he said, punctuating his request with several more profane words. Clara and I quickly steered Annie and Charlie back to the library. I also needed to get out of the hall in a hurry to get over a fit of the giggles. I didn't think Wykeham would appreciate giggles at such a time.

We were composed and sitting quite primly in the library by the time he came in the library door, still dusting off his coat. It was the worse for wear and a shoulder seam was ripped. "Oh, dear," Clara said, leaping for her needle. "Do take off your coat and let me mend it."

"That isn't necessary," Wykeham assured her with a smile. "It's only a minor rent."

Actually, the tear was about seven or eight inches long, but I didn't say a word. Clara was distressed enough as it was. Charlie, however, wasn't concerned about his waistcoat. She, to my horror, leaped up on his lap and gave him a hug. "Did you bring me anything?" she demanded. I reached to remove her, but Wykeham waved me away.

"Yes, I did, you incorrigible urchin," he said, removing two small packets from his waistcoat pocket. "I also brought something for Annie, but neither of you can open your presents until you're ready to get into bed."

Annie managed a very creditable thank-you and a curtsy before she left us, but Charlie snatched her packet and ran for the door. She stopped and finally remembered her manners. "Good night," she said, then ran out the door and up the steps.

"Well," I said, looking on in amazement, "this is a first. No one has ever managed to get Charlie to go to bed without a fight. What on earth did you bring her?"

"She asked me to bring her some ribbons from London," he said, "and, of course, I was glad to oblige. I brought Annie the same thing. Lack of imagination on my part, I suppose, but I know from experience with my sisters that I'm always safe with ribbons."

I stared. "Ribbons? Charlie? Good heavens, why didn't she ask me for some? There's no reason to bother you with a request for ribbons. Whatever could she want with them?"

"Stop, stop!" he said with a laugh. "I imagine she wants ribbons because she's growing up, and I also imagine ribbons from London would be better in her eyes than whatever you could buy in the village. Besides, I offered."

"Nice of you," I said with a smile. "I appreciate it."

"I did it because I wanted to," he said.

I nodded. "I know that. It's just that you seem to want to do the nicest things for our family. It's an unusual experience for us."

There was a short pause before I collected myself enough to ask if he wanted me to ring for tea. "No, Lord, no," he groaned. "I've had enough tea to do me a lifetime. Is there any coffee in the house?"

I rang for Jervis and sent for coffee. Clara said she wanted to see about the girls and asked to be excused. Wykeham detained her. "I didn't mean to slight you, Miss Conroy," he said with a smile that had her beaming. "I brought you a present, as well." With that he produced a book that had a somewhat lurid-looking cover. Clara gave a little scream of delight and thanked him so profusely that I thought she was going to fall at his feet. Then she, too, rushed out of the room and I surmised she was dashing up to her chamber to spend the night reading the latest romance.

"You're going to be the downfall of old ladies," I told Wykeham as I poured his coffee. "And young ones, as well" I added, remembering his effect on Charlie.

"What about the middle ones?" he asked with a grin.

"I don't know any middle ones," I told him, "unless you count Babs. I'm sure she would be quite head over heels with you if she were here."

He laughed aloud, a deep, rich sound. I always enjoyed hearing him laugh. "I can now see myself cutting a swath through London society," he said. "Boorish American manners may become all the rage."

I looked up in alarm. "Boorish manners? Whoever told you such a thing?"

"No one," he said with a sideways look at me. "It's just something we rebel whelps have to live with."

I choked and almost dropped my cup. "Oh, good heavens, where did you hear about that? You must realize that poor Papa never knew what a fine person you were. He would have . . ." My voice trailed off when I couldn't think of anything else to say.

"Actually, I thought being labeled a damned rebel whelp

was funny, and in answer to your first question, David told me."

"I should have known," I muttered. It was time to change the subject. "What did you find out in London about the robbery?" I asked subtly. "Rebeckah told me you had gone up to confer with the Runners about it."

"Is nothing ever secret around this place?" he demanded.

"Nothing," I answered promptly. "Now, what did you discover?"

He shrugged. "Not as much as I had hoped. What I did find out was more disturbing than substantial. Peverell is going to follow up an excellent lead and let me know. I told him I'd probably be in London very soon." He glanced at me. "Rebeckah tells me that you're determined to go to London to wed Harry."

I couldn't meet his eyes. "Yes," I said, looking at a point directly over his shoulder. "I've quite made up my mind."

He hesitated. "Here are my boorish American manners again, but Rebeckah and I want to be there. She tells me we're invited, but I wanted to make sure."

"Of course, you are. I want both of you there," I said, forcing a smile. "I hope my whole family will be in attendance."

He rose. "I plan to be. Let me know a day or so in advance, if you will."

"I plan to leave day after tomorrow."

He looked at me in surprise. "That soon? I suppose it has been almost a fortnight since you told me you were going to do this." He came over and took my hand, pulling me up. "I want to be there with you, and if you decide to change your mind, I want you to know that I'll be right there." He stared at me intently. "You don't *have* to do this if you don't want to."

I forced myself to look right into those turquoise eyes. "I want to," I said firmly. I thought my knees were going to buckle.

"All right," he said, dropping my hand. "Rebeckah and I will be there with you."

I managed a laugh. "You make my wedding sound more like a funeral," I said.

To my surprise, he didn't laugh. He merely looked intently at me again and nodded. "Perhaps," he said, walking toward the door. There he turned and flashed a smile at me. "Good night, Frankie."

I started to say good night in return, but he was gone, and I heard Jervis let him out the front door. Wearily, I sank back into my chair, busying myself by stacking the coffee cups on the tray in front of me. Why, I wondered, did Wykeham always make me feel that marrying Harry wasn't what I wanted to do? When I was with him, I never thought of Harry—never thought of spending the rest of my life with him. Actually, what I wanted to do was spend the rest of my life with Wykeham.

"Good God!" I said aloud as I dropped a cup and watched it shatter at my feet. Did I truly care about him? It simply couldn't be. I was only remembering Clara's silly suggestions about us. I was in love with Harry. I had been in love with him for years. Surely, what I felt for Harry was love. It had to be. The way I felt was. . . . I groped for words, but there were none.

At any rate, I could never be in love with Wykeham. Besides, I thought bitterly, placing his cup carefully on the tray next to the fragments of mine, he would never care about me. I could still hear him whispering, calling for Nancy.

No, for me he was a friend, nothing more.

Wasn't he?

Chapter 15

The next morning was as gray as my spirits. Even Clara was subdued, but considering her bloodshot eyes, I decided it was from staying up all night reading her novel. Only Charlie seemed to consider the day fit for living. Annie whined so much that I let her go spend a few days with one of her friends in the village. That done, I enlisted both Charlie and Clara to help me pack my things for London, and to help me make sure my clothes were presentable. I thought this would pull me out of the doldrums, but every single thing that went in the trunk made me feel that much worse. I was beginning to feel as if I were going into exile.

Late in the morning, there was a great clatter outside, followed by a shout. Then we heard more shouting and a banging on the door. Clara and I quickly looked out my window and saw a heavily lathered horse being taken away by a groom.

"Could something have happened to Wykeham?" I asked without thinking. "His health . . ." I let the words dangle off.

"No." Clara shook her head. "No, that horse has traveled far—probably from London."

I looked at her and we ran for the door and dashed down the stairs, almost colliding with Jervis on the first landing. When we finally untangled ourselves, Jervis handed me an envelope. "An urgent message for you from your sister, the messenger said. I've sent him to the kitchen, and his horse to the stables."

"Very good, Jervis," I said, my fingers itching to open the envelope. Instead, I took it back up to the room and closed the door behind me. If it was bad news, I didn't wish to break down in front of Clara and Charlie. I would tell them about it in a dignified manner.

I tore open the envelope and shrieked aloud when I read it. Clara and Charlie ignored the closed door and came tumbling into the room. "What is it?" Clara gasped.

"It's from Lizzie," I said, collapsing on the edge of my bed amid all my clothes. "Babs has eloped."

" 'Loped?" Charlie was puzzled. "Is that bad?"

"Oh dear, how very romantic," Clara said.

I stared at them for a moment. "Romantic?" I finally sputtered. "This is a catastrophe. Lizzie didn't tell me who the man was, so I suspect the worst. He's probably an actor or something." I jumped to my feet. "I've got to go to London right away. There may still be time to do something. An annulment might be possible." I started throwing clothes around and aiming for my trunk. "Help me, Clara. I'll just take the necessary items."

"Shouldn't you notify the earl?" Clara asked, dragging a portmanteau into the middle of the floor. "Considering the way he feels about his responsibilities, I'm sure he'd want to know."

"No, he doesn't need to know this." I paused. "He *will* want to know, won't he?" I ran for the landing. "Jervis," I yelled down the stairs, "Please find Griggins and send him to me."

"Very well, milady," Jervis said from right behind me. "I'll tell him to take a message to the earl."

I didn't take time to tell Jervis he shouldn't eavesdrop, but went straight to the library to scribble a quick note to Wykeham. With any luck, I could be gone within an hour or two and I would have fulfilled my obligations to Wykeham. He didn't need to try to sort this out—it was entirely my responsibility.

I had just finished putting on my traveling dress when Wykeham burst into my room. "What's going on?" he demanded.

"I'm getting dressed," I said. "Really, you shouldn't come in like this."

"Sorry," he said, not meaning it at all. He shoved some gowns aside and sat on the edge of my bed, looking at my jumbled portmanteau. "You're going to London?"

"Right away. I got a letter from Lizzie that Babs has eloped. I don't know who the man is—probably some actor," I said bitterly.

"I think you're closer to being right than you realize," he said grimly. "I'm going with you. I'll go back to Foxcroft and pack a few things. You can come by there and get me."

"You don't—" I began.

"Yes, I do. I might have prevented this if I had only . . ." He stopped. "I'm afraid there might be bad news for you, and I need to be there. I don't want to hear any arguments."

He didn't get any arguments from me—I didn't have time to argue, as he was already out the door. "Stop!" I yelled, dashing for the door. "Tell me what you know." He was already down the stairs. "Later," he called back over his shoulder.

I was thoroughly puzzled. I wanted to find out why he thought he might have prevented Babs's elopement, but that would have to wait until the journey to London. And *what* was that he had said about Babs running off with an actor?

When we pulled up in front of Foxcroft, Wykeham threw his bag in the boot and peered into the carriage. "Are you all right?"

"I'm fine," I snapped. "What else would you expect?"

"Good," he said, unperturbed by my sarcasm. "I'm going to ride on the box." With that, he hoisted himself up with the coachman and sent Griggins back to ride with me. I immediately decided he had ridden up front to keep from talking to me. He knew me well enough to know I would interrogate him.

Griggins leaned back and closed his eyes as we got underway, while I sat in the carriage and pondered all sides of Wykeham's recent conversations with me. I couldn't see what he could possibly know about Babs—unless, the thought came to me, it was somehow connected with something the Runners had learned. But that was ridiculous. Babs might go head over heels about some handsome stripling, or even half a dozen of them, but she would never become involved with a thief.

We stopped for a quick nuncheon, and then continued at a good clip. Neither Wykeham or I wanted to waste any time. There was another quick stop for a rather bad dinner of boiled mutton. I had planned to quiz Wykeham then, but the only place for us to eat was a table in the common room. I thought he was rather relieved. He paid our reckoning and I thought he was going to get into the carriage with me. I could see he was stiff and tired. "I promise I won't question you if you want to ride in here," I said, feeling sorry for him.

He flashed me a quick smile. "I know you better than that," he said, shutting the door and getting ready to climb up with the coachman. In a moment we were underway, on into the dark. It was almost midnight by the time we arrived at the London house.

"I can't stay here," I told Wykeham as he came around to the carriage door. "It would be all over London that you and I had stayed here without a chaperone. Harry would be scandalized."

"Damn Harry," Wykeham said shortly. "Very well, I'll take you to Lizzie's then, but I'm ordering you not to do anything until you and I talk together with Lizzie and find out about this."

"You're ordering me?" I tried to sound indignant, but I was too tired.

"Yes. There are some things you might not..." He stopped and put his hand on mine. "Just don't do anything without me. Do you promise?"

I was too weary to argue. "I promise."

The carriage pulled up in front of Lizzie's and Wykeham helped me down. "I'll be here first thing in the morning. In the meantime, remember, you promised." He smiled briefly at me and gave me a quick kiss on the forehead. I caught my breath, stared at him, and started to speak, but he was already getting into the carriage. He gave me a smile as they drove away.

I didn't have time to wonder why he had acted that way, or why I was still so breathless. The door was flung open and Lizzie grabbed me around the neck. "Oh, Frankie!" she wailed. "Isn't it terrible?"

I pulled her from my neck and managed to shove her back inside. "It's past terrible. Will you stop drenching me and tell me exactly what happened?"

Lizzie stopped and looked at me in surprise. "I thought *you* knew."

"How could I know, Lizzie? You're the one who was responsible for Babs here in London. All I know is what you wrote to me."

"But Babs wrote that you would know." Lizzie seemed thoroughly confused.

"Babs left a letter, then?" Lizzie nodded and I took her firmly by the arm. "Show it to me."

Lizzie led the way to her library and took a much-crumpled sheet of paper from the desk drawer. "I just don't know how this could have happened," she sniffled, handing it to me.

I glanced over Babs's scrawl. "Lizzie, she says here that she's run away with the most wonderful man in the world," I said, frowning as I tried to decipher Babs's handwriting.

"Look at the next line," Lizzie wailed. "She writes that you'll know exactly what she's talking about."

I sat down and felt my throbbing head. "I certainly don't know what she means. Of course, it isn't often that anyone knows what Babs is saying."

"What are we going to do?" Lizzie wailed.

I glared up at her. "Hush that, Lizzie. There isn't anything we can do at this time of night. Wykeham will be here first thing in the morning, and then we'll try to find Babs. Perhaps Mademoiselle DeSalle could help us."

"She's gone, too," Lizzie said, sniffling. "She might be with friends or something. She didn't leave a note."

"Are her clothes here?" I asked. Lizzie was as helpless and hysterical as Babs. "Did you look?"

"I wouldn't want to go through her things, Frankie."

"I would," I snapped. "Show me to her room."

As I had expected, Mademoiselle DeSalle's room was quite bare. I also checked in the room Babs had occupied. All her clothing was gone as well. "Lizzie, how could you not have noticed that the two of them were leaving? They must have had two or three trunks between them. Surely, you saw something."

She shook her head. "No, I went to a ball that night and stayed in bed until after noon. When I asked about Babs, one of the maids told me she had gone out. I did ask about her clothes when I found the letter—I really did, Frankie. She and Mademoiselle had hired a boy to carry them down the back way into a carriage."

"Well, that's something. What time did they leave?"

Lizzie looked quite miserable. "I was still abed. The maid told me they left early, before ten. I looked all over for them all day yesterday, and then I wrote to you."

"You looked all day *yesterday*?" I felt utterly defeated. "Lizzie, are you telling me that Babs has been missing for *two* days?"

She nodded. "I kept thinking she'd return and there was no point in worrying you. You know how Babs does these things for effect."

"Full well I know," I said grimly. "If she's been gone for two days, even Wykeham might not be able to do anything." I wearily walked to the door. "Just show me to a bed, Lizzie. Wykeham will be here tomorrow and perhaps we can begin to search. I'm afraid it's too late to salvage her reputation."

"How will I ever live this down?" Lizzie was wailing again. "You know my mother-in-law is a paragon of propriety."

I was quite out of sorts with Lizzie. "You'll simply have to brazen it out," I said shortly. "Now, if you'll stop having hysterics and show me a bed, I'd appreciate it. We'll meet with Wykeham in the morning. Surely he'll know what we can do."

Lizzie sent her maid in to me the next morning, and she did as much as was humanly possible, but when I examined myself in the mirror, I still looked wretched—exactly like someone who had received a blow and hadn't slept at all. "Fitting," I mumbled to myself.

Wykeham was already downstairs having a cup of coffee in the breakfast room when I got down. I inquired about Lizzie and was told she was still abed. I sent someone up to wake her and fetch her downstairs so Wykeham could talk to her.

"What did Lizzie tell you?" he asked briefly, pouring me a cup of coffee. "Here, you need this."

I drank a big gulp of it, and gave him a quick summary of everything Lizzie had said, emphasizing that they had been gone for days now. I showed him the note Babs had written. "I can't imagine what she means," I told him. "She says I should know exactly about this most wonderful man."

Wykeham reached over and took my hand. "I've been up since daylight and have made several inquiries," he said. "I thought I had some information leading up to this, but I wanted to confirm my suspicions." He stopped and looked searchingly at me. "Frankie, I really don't know how to do this except to come right out and say it. It appears that Babs . . ." He stopped, seemingly unsure of himself.

"Go on," I prompted. "Nothing you can tell me about Babs will surprise me."

"It's not only about Babs," he said. "Frankie," he began, then took a deep breath. "My dear, I don't want to hurt you, but I must tell you. There seems to be no doubt about it—Babs has eloped with Harry."

For a second I didn't move. Then, the room began spinning crazily around me. "I'm sorry," I managed to say. "I thought you said Harry."

Wykeham got up and poured me some brandy in a glass. "Here," he said. "It's a little early for this, but you need it." He put the glass in my hand and moved it up to my lips. "It's true—Babs and Harry have eloped."

I sipped at the hot liquid, then tipped the glass up and drained it. I choked and there were tears in my eyes, but at least it made the room stop spinning.

Wykeham sat down beside me again. "I'm sorry, Frankie. When I was in London before, I had information that Harry was seeing Babs, but, for your sake, I was hoping he was being a brother to her." He paused, and his knuckles were white on the table's edge. "Evidently I was wrong."

"Evidently we were both wrong about Harry," I said dully. "What else did you discover? Lizzie tells me Babs has been missing for two days—three now."

He nodded. "My sources tell me that Harry met two fashionably dressed women down at the docks about mid-morning day before yesterday and they took a boat for France. They had two or three trunks with them."

"Babs and Mademoiselle," I said. "Who told you?"

"Peverell." He hesitated again. "I suppose I should tell you the whole story. I've carried this around with me and I've wanted to, but dammit—" He crashed his fist into the table. "Frankie, I didn't know what to do, what to say. I couldn't say anything to you without definite proof, and I didn't have enough to be sure. I didn't want to hurt you, and you were so set on marrying Harry."

I looked at him. "Tell me," I said quietly. "It's my right to know everything."

He glanced around to make sure no servants were near.

"Let's go somewhere private," he suggested. "Does this house have a library or a study?"

I nodded and got up. He grabbed the brandy decanter and another glass and followed me to the library. Once there, I closed the door firmly behind me and sat down, feigning a calm I didn't feel. "All right, tell me."

He sat down across from me and pulled his chair closer to mine, so he could reach over and take my hands. "I knew how you felt about Harry," he said, "and I was hoping everything I was learning was wrong, but there seems no doubt now." He looked bitter. "Actually, my inquiries might have been one of the spurs to force Harry's hand now, instead of waiting until you two were married."

"Why were you asking about Harry?" I asked. "Did you not trust my judgment?"

"Oh, no, that wasn't it at all," he said hastily. "Harry wasn't even a consideration, at first, and didn't come into things until fairly late in the game." He dropped my hands and stood, pacing the floor with his hands in his pockets. "Peverell had been working on the robbery and had several excellent leads. He had even managed to locate some of the loot—several pictures and a silver tea set. In every case, the description of the person who had sold the stolen goods matched that of Harry Apsley."

"Harry! I don't believe it for a moment." I looked up at Wykeham. "Peverell has to be wrong about this. Harry might do many things, but he would never steal."

He paused and bit his lip, then leaned against the mantel. "That's what I kept telling myself, and Peverell, as well. English gentlemen might gamble or chase a lightskirt, but overall, they're an honorable lot. I kept on saying this until Peverell managed to run the Skeltons to earth." Wykeham pulled an envelope from his waistcoat pocket. "Here's a copy of a letter the Skeltons wrote in front of a magistrate, swearing that Harry masterminded the whole robbery and gave them a cut of the proceeds to let him in the house."

I was stunned and couldn't speak for a moment. "It's hard to believe," I finally said. "Harry was constantly without a feather to fly with, and he told me his father was tight with the purse strings, but I can't believe he would resort to robbery."

"Evidently he did," Wykeham said grimly. "After Peverell gave me this, I asked him to investigate Harry's background. I was worried by then because you were determined to marry him."

"And you found that his background was not as he said?" My words were flat. I could just imagine Harry as a young boy doing risky things—things that became more illegal as time went on. I knew Harry well enough to know that he would thrive on a hint of risk, and he would never believe he could be caught.

He nodded. "From what Peverell could discover, Harry has indulged the dark side of his nature. He's been involved in several illegal affairs since he's been in London, and things were even worse when he was in the islands." Wykeham came back over and sat down next to me. "Evidently Harry's father knew something of his past and had given him an ultimatum: to marry you or be disowned."

"To marry me." The meaning gradually sunk in. "Then, Harry was only marrying me to satisfy his father. He never cared at all."

He took my hands. "I'm sorry, sweetheart."

"Don't pity me," I said. I was fighting back tears.

He reached up and wiped a tear from my cheek. "I don't pity you, Frankie. I'm sorry I had to be the one to hurt you so. If anyone, I pity Babs."

"You didn't hurt me," I told him. "I'd rather know now than after it was too late. But why Babs? Why would Harry talk her into eloping with him?"

"He needed the money," he said bluntly. "I was making arrangements so that your marriage portion would be safe from him. Since Harry married Babs, whatever she has is his now. She has a very handsome settlement from her mother, aside from her marriage portion. I can't control that at all. Actually, from Harry's point of view, Babs is a much better financial arrangement than you were."

"That's wonderful to know," I said dully. "You have a very fine way of saying things."

He tried a smile. "I'm not very good with the flowery

phrase, am I? I do mean well, Frankie, and you know I'd never do or say anything to hurt you.''

I smiled back at him—a weak and wobbly smile. ''I know that. Is there anything at all we can do for Babs at this point?''

He frowned. ''I don't think we can do anything about the marriage if it's already been performed and, uh . . .''

''Consummated,'' I supplied.

''Yes. And knowing Harry, I assume that's the case.''

I nodded. ''I agree. We're already too late. Is there anything you can do to make her life with Harry better? I'm afraid he'll abandon her as soon as he goes through her inheritance.''

''I'll see what I can do,'' he promised. ''Now, in the meantime . . .''

He was interrupted by Lizzie, hurtling through the library door. ''Do you have news? Have you found her?'' she cried, making a very fetching picture by standing and wringing her hands. I noted that she had taken the time to dress and have her maid fix her hair. There was even a spot of rouge on her cheeks. ''Tell me, please tell me!'' she wailed, collapsing on a nearby chair.

''Good Lord, Lizzie,'' I said. ''You're as bad as Babs ever was. Get hold of yourself.'' I waited until she had sat up in her chair and stopped the melodramatics. ''Babs has eloped with Harry,'' I told her, feigning a calm I certainly didn't feel. ''It seems they've gone to France, along with three trunks and Mademoiselle DeSalle.''

Lizzie's mouth fell open. ''No!''

''I'm afraid so,'' I said. ''Wykeham has been making inquiries and that seems to be the case.''

''So that's why she said you would know about the man. Why didn't you tell me, Frankie?''

I gave her a disgusted look. ''I didn't know about it. *You* were the one responsible for her in London—you should have known about it. I can't believe you let her form such an attachment.''

Lizzie didn't even hear me. ''I shall never live through this,'' she moaned, covering her face with her hands. ''I'll never be able to show my face in public again.''

"Nonsense," I told her. "I doubt that anyone cares. Why don't you write your mother-in-law and tell her, so she doesn't find out from anyone else."

"Better than that," Lizzie said, jumping up. "I'll go see her and tell her myself."

"Fine," I said, but Lizzie was already halfway out the door.

Suddenly she stopped and turned to look at me, a puzzled look on her face. "I thought *you* were going to marry Harry," she said.

It was too much. I started laughing hysterically and couldn't stop. Then my laughter turned into tears, and they wouldn't stop either. Wykeham poured a full glass of brandy down me, sloshing a great deal of it on my gown in the process, and made me walk back and forth across the floor. Finally, I managed to control myself, but I was still hiccuping.

"It's the brandy," I said between hiccups as I sat back down in my chair.

"Why don't you go upstairs and go back to bed?" Wykeham asked. He mopped ineffectually with his handkerchief at some brandy on my chin. "You'll feel better after you rest a bit, and truly, there's nothing else you can do."

I shook my head. "Yes, there is. I'm going back to Foxcroft."

"You really can't . . ." he begun, then paused. "You're quite right. That might be the very best thing for you, Frankie. There's been no announcement of your engagement to Harry, and there's no need for anyone to know what's actually happened. We'll go back today if you wish."

"You don't have to go," I said, still hiccuping. "I can go by myself. You stay in London if you want."

"I want to take you back. After all, we came all this way unchaperoned, and I don't think anyone will know if we return the same way. We can be back at the Dower House by midnight, if you're game."

"You're too good to me," I said, spouting fresh tears. "I'll be ready to leave within half an hour—I haven't even unpacked yet."

He patted my hand. "Good. I'll check with Peverell and leave a few instructions, then come by and get you. I'll be back in about an hour—earlier, if I can manage it." He walked to the library door, then stopped to look back at me. "Are you sure you're all right?"

I hiccuped. "Fine. All I want to do is go home. I'll go tell Lizzie."

Lizzie wailed and moaned that I was leaving her alone to face the scandal, and mentioned various other responsibilities that I was forcing her to face alone. I told her she was ridiculous.

"Furthermore, Lizzie," I told her, "if you don't say anything about this, I don't think the word will travel far. I know Harry's father will try to keep this quiet, especially when he hears about Harry."

"What about Harry?" Lizzie asked. I had forgotten she didn't know about Harry's part in the robbery.

"I'll have to talk to Wykeham before I say anything else. In the meantime, go visit your mother-in-law and tell her how delighted we are that Babs has married the heir to Mountnorris."

"But, we're not delighted," Lizzie said.

"I know that, you goose, and you know that, but the *ton* doesn't, and if we can pretend we're delighted, who's going to know? It's up to you to pull it off, Lizzie."

"To me?" Lizzie looked dubious, then squared her shoulders. "Of course, I can do that." She looked at me. "The *ton* will believe anything."

I left on that note, meeting Wykeham in the hall, and we set out for Foxcroft. This time, he rode in the carriage with me, and told me stories about his life in America to distract me. His consideration amazed me—he was so understanding. For a fleeting moment I wished things had been different—that there had been no Harry and no Nancy. But that hadn't been, and Wykeham and I would forever be only friends.

Chapter 16

Wykeham had been wrong about one thing: it wasn't midnight when we arrived at the Dower House—it was well after. The moon was out and it was a clear night, so we were able to travel. I was worried about traveling so late at night, but Wykeham said we could do it, and we did, although I own I was completely exhausted. I finally realized that he was cured—anyone who could withstand that trip had to be in the best of health.

When we got to the Dower House, I roused the household enough to get the door opened, and Wykeham and Griggins piled my luggage on the floor of the hall. We said good night, and I went up to bed, leaving my luggage to be sorted out in the morning. I met Clara on the stairs and briefly told her what had happened. I should have known better—she immediately flung herself on my neck and began weeping. "Oh, you poor dear," she mumbled over and over, patting me on the head. It took me fully five minutes to disengage her.

"Please, Clara, I need to get some sleep," I said, holding her at arm's length.

"Oh, or course, you poor little dear," she said. "How very thoughtless of me. You just go on to bed, and I'll go right down and warm you a glass of milk. It's just what you need to make you sleep."

Before I could tell her that all I needed to sleep was a bed and some quiet, she was off down the stairs, humming to herself. Clara was born to fuss over someone. Resigned, I went on to my room, undressed, and crawled into bed. Clara came in on tiptoe, carrying my warm milk, and put it beside me. She shook my shoulder to make sure I knew it was there, and then tiptoed out again. There was only one thing to do and I did it: I turned the glass up and drained it. I loathe warm milk.

I slept until noon the next day. When I finally woke and went downstairs, Clara told me Wykeham had been by to check on me and would be back in the evening. I could see that she was dying to hear all the small details, but I didn't want to discuss it. After several not-so-subtle hints I gave up, gritted my teeth, and told her everything. That is, almost everything: I omitted Harry's part in the robbery.

"The villain!" she said. "To mislead you and that other poor child!" She clenched her small fists. "Oh, if I had him here, I'd teach him some manners! I'd ... I'd ... why, I'd box his ears!"

"I imagine Wykeham will do that when he next sees Harry," I told her. "He has some other scores to settle with him as well."

"He's such a wonderful man," Clara said dreamily. "So handsome, just like the hero in ..." She caught herself and blushed.

"You *do* mean Wykeham and not Harry, I hope."

Clara gave me an astonished look. "Certainly I'm talking about the earl. After all, I never thought you should marry that other scoundrel. I knew what he was in the first place." She nodded her head wisely at me. "I know the type."

I doubted that Clara had had much experience with Harry's type, but I let the conversation drop. Evidently, everyone except me had known what Harry was. Just to get away, I dragooned Griggins into helping me and we went back out to the digs to uncover our trenches. I was determined to begin again, and this time I meant to finish. I would uncover the entire villa and write that up, as well. In the meantime, I would polish my paper some more so that Wykeham could present it. He was scheduled to speak to the Society at its meeting the next month. It would be exciting if I were to discover something else by then.

We didn't hear from Harry and Babs, and I tried my best to stop thinking about them. Over the next three weeks I threw myself entirely into my work. I was up early and finished late. Evenings were spent either with Clara, Annie, and Charlie in the library while I worked on my paper, or else with Wykeham and Rebeckah at Foxcroft. On those evenings, David and Rebeckah sat and talked quietly, holding hands, of course, while Wykeham and I played chess. I made every effort to put Harry out of my mind, and I was slowly succeeding. I realized I had never loved him, but the elopement with Babs was a blow to my pride. Getting over that was the hard part.

One Friday evening, I arrived at Foxcroft even later than usual. I had planned to dine with Rebeckah, Wykeham, and David, but David had a medical emergency in the village, and Rebeckah had decided to stay with David's mother until he returned. When I received Wykeham's note to that effect, I dined with Clara and the girls, waiting until rather late to go over to Foxcroft for our usual chess game. It was dark by the time Griggins and I started for the manor. The moon was only on the quarter, so Griggins walked beside me, carrying a lantern. I was engrossed in discussing my plans for the next week at the digs, and didn't see the man in the path until we were well on him.

"Out for an evening stroll?"

I gasped. "Harry! What are you doing here?" I glanced at Griggins, who had put the lantern down and adopted a pose suitable for the boxing ring. "That won't be necessary, Griggins," I said hastily. "Please wait over there for a moment." I waited until Griggins had gotten out of earshot. I noted he was standing warily, waiting to spring. Evidently, Harry wasn't now one of Griggins's favorite people.

"What is the meaning of this, Harry?" I demanded. "What have you done with Babs?"

"She's quite safe, I assure you. She's with my father. I'm happy to say they seem to be getting along famously—much better than I ever got along with him."

"Did you wed her?" I bit the words off.

I could see Harry's expression in the faint light from the lantern. He smiled a twisted smile at me. "Of course I did, Frankie. I told you I had to get married right away."

"You don't care at all for Babs, do you, Harry?" I paused. "You never cared at all for me, either, did you?" I tried to hide it, but my voice was bitter. "I couldn't see it until now, but you've never cared at all for anyone except yourself."

"Of course I cared for you, Frankie," he said smoothly, reaching for my hand and letting his fingers wander familiarly up my wrist.

I jerked my hand away from him. "Don't touch me, Harry. I swear I'll kill you if you do."

He threw his head back and laughed. "Quite the firebrand, aren't you, Frankie? That's what I've always liked about you."

"You're despicable, Harry. Perhaps you never cared for me, but I've discovered that I didn't care for you, either. I was enthralled by the idea of being in love, but I know now that I didn't love you. I never have."

He looked at me strangely. "Oh, and have you discovered true love?" His face twisted and he grasped my wrist, hurting me. "I suppose you've set your sights on Wykeham. Keeping it all in the family, aren't you?"

"I don't know what you're talking about," I told him, pulling back. I was afraid I was going to have to call for Griggins.

"Don't play coy with me, Frankie," Harry snarled. "I saw how the wind blew a long time ago, and that's one of the reasons I settled on Babs. Wykeham wasn't about to let you marry me. He wants you for himself."

I stood straight and stared at him. "That's ridiculous. All you're doing is making excuses for your shortcomings. You married Babs for her money. You would have married me for the same reason, but Wykeham blocked you." I stepped back and tried to control my anger. "You're not half the man he is, Harry. You never will be. You can't even go face him now because you're afraid of him."

Harry's face twisted almost into a snarl. "Afraid? Do you really think I'm afraid of that provincial bumpkin? By God, I'll show you." He grabbed my wrist again and started down the path to Foxcroft, pulling me in his wake. "Griggins," I called, trying in vain to keep the alarm out of my voice, "follow us."

I had difficulty keeping up with Harry, and by the time we reached Foxcroft, he was practically dragging me up the steps. My wrist hurt dreadfully, but I was afraid to say anything for fear Griggins would try to take my part. Harry let me go while he banged on the door, cursing and calling out to Wykeham to let us in. Brooks opened the door, looking quite startled. I was glad to see Perkins standing behind him, looking as menacing as usual.

"Tell the earl that Harry Apsley is here to see him,"

Harry demanded. "Lady Frances is here with me, and we don't choose to wait."

Brooks escorted us inside and walked to the library. Harry didn't wait to be announced but walked right behind him, shoving him aside and entering the library, dragging me behind him. Wykeham was sitting near one of the garden windows, reading, the chessboard ready beside him. "Hello, Wykeham," Harry said with an unpleasant smile. "I've come to discuss some business with you, and happened to run into a friend of mine." He put an arm around my shoulder and I ducked to get away. I put a chair between us. Harry's very touch made me shudder.

Wykeham stood up very calmly. "Where's Babs, Harry?"

Harry laughed harshly and sprawled out in a chair, reaching for Wykeham's decanter of brandy and a glass. He poured himself a healthy portion. "I left my blushing bride with my father. I needed to come talk to you about advancing me her marriage settlement. You and I didn't manage to have this conversation before the ceremony."

"You did marry her, then?"

Harry pulled a document out of his coat pocket and flipped it toward Wykeham. "Read it for yourself," he said.

Wykeham glanced over the document. "It looks all right to me," he said. "I'm glad you had the sense to marry her immediately."

Harry shrugged. "No matter. Now, about the money. . ."

"That's been taken care of already but it is Babs's money, and you are not to touch it," Wykeham said evenly. "I informed your father of my decision and he was in complete agreement."

Harry sat up so quickly his glass fell to the floor and rolled on the carpet, leaving a stain where the brandy splattered. "But I'm her husband!" he said, choking.

"Yes and if I ever hear you have touched a penny of it, you'll be very sorry," Wykeham said, not raising his voice. He walked over to his desk and pulled out three large envelopes. "I, too, have some interesting documents, Harry." He held up the first one. "This one is a sworn statement from the Skeltons that you were the mastermind behind the robbery of the London house."

Harry stiffened and turned deathly pale for a moment. Then he took a deep breath and forced himself to look at Wykeham and smile. "No one would believe that," he said with a shrug. "Everyone will simply think you're trying to trap me."

"Be that as it may," Wykeham said, his voice level. He held up the second envelope. "In this envelope are sworn statements from a man who handled your stolen goods. He's implicated you not only with the robbery of my house in London, but with robberies in several other houses. While he was being questioned by Peverell and the Runners, he incidentally gave evidence that you were engaged in illegal activities in the islands."

"You can't prove a thing," Harry said hoarsely. He was trying to stay calm as he faced Wykeham, but I noticed his hands were shaking.

"Oh, I think I can, Harry," Wykeham said. He held up the third envelope. "In this envelope is a letter to your father, outlining all your illegal activities. There is also a letter to be given to the authorities in the event anything unusual happens to me." He paused. "I think everything in here is well documented, and, of course, these are only copies. The originals are in a bank vault, there's another copy with Banks, my solicitor."

"You wouldn't use them. You wouldn't dare." Harry gave up all pretense of calm. He was chalk white and his voice was trembling.

"Oh, certainly I would," Wykeham said, almost pleasantly. "But I don't intend to right now." He walked over to Harry. "Of course, I'm sure you realize there's a price for my silence."

"How much?" Harry gasped.

Wykeham looked at him much as one might look at a particularly repulsive insect. "Not money, Harry. You couldn't buy me for any price. No, I have something else in mind." He paused. "You're going to settle in the country with Babs and be a model husband, Harry. You're going to make Babs the happiest wife in England. If you don't, I'll use every one of these documents."

"You wouldn't do that to Babs," Harry said. "I know you wouldn't want that kind of scandal in the family."

"Do you want to try me, Harry?" Wykeham's voice was as cold as ice. I almost didn't recognize it.

Harry sat in a stony silence that seemed to last forever. Finally, Wykeham came over to him. "Are we in agreement, then?" he asked pleasantly, almost as if he were discussing the weather. "I expect you to live up to your part of the bargain, or I promise you, I'll use everything I have against you and damn the consequences."

"You'd regret the consequences, Wykeham," Harry snarled. "I could hurt you, you know."

"I don't think so," Wykeham said smoothly.

Harry laughed—a short, harsh sound. "Oh, yes." He glanced over at me. "I could have had her any time I wanted to." His mouth twisted in a parody of a smile. "Do you think I was such a fool that I didn't notice how you felt? I saw you looking at her, and I knew what you wanted." Harry stood in front of Wykeham. "And maybe I still might have her. How would you like that?"

Wykeham grasped the edge of the chair until his knuckles turned white. He was pale with the effort of controlling himself. "Get out of here, Apsley, before I lose my temper with you. You're not worth hanging for or, by God, I'd kill you where you stand."

Harry laughed again, an unpleasant sound. "Think about what I said, Wykeham. I might be around any time. In the meantime, I'll take you up on your offer and retire to the country, but don't feel too secure." He passed by me on his way out and reached out to touch my arm.

I shrank away from him. "Stay away from me, Harry." My voice was as shaky as my knees.

"You never could resist me, Frankie," he said with a chuckle as he went out the door. "I don't think you'll be able to resist later. At my convenience." I couldn't stop myself from reaching over and slamming the door behind him. I felt drained. I went over to one of the chairs and collapsed in it.

"Was all that true, Wykeham?" I asked as he sat down beside me. "About the envelopes and the evidence, I mean."

He nodded. "All that and more. I don't know how long he'll stay with Babs, but I think his father will see to it that he behaves himself and makes her a decent husband. To his credit, he knows what kind of son he has." He reached over and took my hand. "I'm just sorry that you had to hear all this, but I wanted someone in the family to know, in case anything happened to me."

"I'm glad I know." I stopped a moment. "I never loved him. I thought I did, but I was . . ." I groped for a word. "I was infatuated with someone who didn't exist anymore—someone I knew when I was sixteen. Maybe that Harry didn't exist even then." I paused and bit my lip as I tried to sort things out. "But why did he come back here and want to marry me? Was it for the money?"

Wykeham moved his chair close to mine and took my other hand, as well. "Partially. Harry was dipped rather deeply, but he was selling enough stolen goods to keep going. As for getting married, I told you his father had given him an ultimatum—marry you or be disowned. In order to get any money out of his father, Harry had to come up with a bride—and the bride's portion wouldn't hurt any. When you kept putting him off, Harry got desperate and married Babs instead. There was an added attraction in that she also had, if you'll forgive me, a better marriage portion than you have." He gave me a quick smile.

"Poor Babs," I said. "Her life won't be what she hoped."

He smiled at me again. "I don't know. I think Harry was bluffing and that he'll do exactly what his father wants him to. He'll settle down and behave himself. Harry's devious, but from what I can discover, he's basically craven. From the little I know of Babs, I think she'll land on her feet."

"I hope so." Harry had said something else I wanted to ask about, but I needed to think about it first. Instead, I found myself blurting it out. "What Harry said . . ."

"Don't worry about it," he said brusquely. "I'll take care of you. Harry knows that."

I bit my lip, worrying with a thought in the back of my mind. "Could you see me home now?" I asked, much to my surprise. It wasn't what I had intended to ask at all.

He stood quickly. "Of course. And I promise you there's no need to worry."

He didn't know it, but Harry was the least of my worries. There was something else on my mind. I had finally managed to put together all the hints that Clara and Rebeckah had given me with what Harry had said. I didn't see how I could have been so stupid—my only excuse was that I didn't know the emotion. I had never been in love before and didn't know how it felt. I wasn't even sure about it now. I needed to think, and that was something I couldn't do in Wykeham's presence.

Chapter 17

Clara was surprised when I returned so early, but I wasn't prepared to tell her anything except that Harry had been at Foxcroft and that Babs was well. Clara thought it quite romantic, and I didn't have the heart to disillusion her. "And did the earl quite put that villain in his place?" she asked as I started to mount the stairs to bed.

"What?" Clara always surprised me by knowing so much more than I thought she did.

"Did the earl put him in his place?" she repeated. "I rather fancied he would."

I smiled at her. "Rest assured that Wykeham took good care of him," I said. "I think Babs will have a model husband." I went on upstairs, leaving Clara to retire with her latest from the Minerva Press. I didn't want to talk to Clara right now—there were times when she was too intuitive.

After a prolonged time of sitting and thinking, looking out the window and thinking, lying on the bed and thinking, and finally, pacing the floor and thinking, I decided to try for a glass of warm milk and a boring book. It was getting close to two o'clock and I hadn't been able to sort out my feelings at all. I also hadn't been able to go to sleep. I went downstairs carefully, shielding my candle, and warmed myself a glass of milk. I looked at it with loathing and carried it to the library, where I lit a branch with my candle and sat down heavily behind my desk. I didn't want to read anything, boring or otherwise. I didn't want to do anything at all except sit and stare numbly at the candle flames.

I was trying bravely to down my glass of warm milk when I heard the library door open. It was Clara. "I thought I heard someone," she said. "Are you ill, my dear?"

Just hopelessly lovesick, I thought to myself. Aloud, I said, "No. I couldn't sleep and got myself a glass of milk. I suppose the excitement of knowing Babs and Harry were back unsettled me."

"Uuummm," Clara said, sitting down in front of the desk where she could see me. She looked at me in the most direct way. "Is there anything you would like to tell me, dear?"

"No," I said shortly, grimacing as I drank some more milk. "I don't know." I paused, wanting to talk but afraid to discuss my feelings. "I'm a little confused."

Clara nodded sagely. "You thought you were in love with that rogue, didn't you?"

I nodded, and she went on. "But you found out that you weren't." I didn't answer, but that didn't stop her. "Now you've discovered true love, haven't you?"

I was in the process of taking another swallow of milk, but at her remark, I choked and had to put the glass down. "I don't know," I mumbled, when I finally caught my breath. "I simply don't know." I stopped and put my hands over my face. "This is ridiculous, Clara. Of course I know. I just don't know what to do about it. I can't just walk up to Wykeham and say that I've decided I love him. He'd go into whoops in a minute."

Clara looked at me. "My dear, don't you know that the man's in love with you? My goodness, he has been for ages. Anyone could have seen it."

"I didn't see it," I said morosely. "And now I've made such a fool of myself over Harry."

"That doesn't signify, not at all," Clara said. "I imagine the earl has made a fool of himself over some woman at one time or the other."

"Nancy," I said bitterly. "There's Nancy."

Clara looked puzzled. "Nancy?"

I gave her a description of Wykeham's whispered words in the sickroom, and told her that Rebeckah had also known about Nancy. To my surprise, Clara laughed aloud. "Oh, my dear, I know about Nancy, as well, and I tell you that the earl prefers you over Nancy. You need have no worries at all about that. And," she continued, "I see no reason why you shouldn't tell the earl how you feel."

"My life isn't one of your books with marbleized covers, Clara," I said somewhat bitterly. "People don't act that way in real life."

"Of course they do," Clara said blithely, standing up. "How would a man know you loved him if you didn't tell him so? People say 'I love you' all the time." She picked up my half full glass of tepid milk and carried it out with her. "I don't really think you need this at all, dear. Go on to bed. Tomorrow will take care of all your worries."

I really didn't think tomorrow would bring anything new, and I didn't think I could sleep, but I did take her advice and go on to bed, protesting all the way. It was midmorning before I woke up.

Clara was downstairs when I went to breakfast. "My dear, I'm sorry to bear bad news," she began, "but . . ."

"Wait until I have some coffee, Clara," I said. "I'm not sure I can take any bad news until then." I poured myself a cup and sat down. "Now," I told her, "do your worst."

She laughed. "It isn't that bad. Wykeham came by this morning. A messenger arrived with a message that his mother was in London. She arrived yesterday, and he and Rebeckah have gone up to get her."

"And Nancy," I said dully, stirring sugar into my coffee. "Rebeckah told me that Nancy was coming with their mother."

"Wonderful," Clara said. I glared at her and spooned some more sugar into my coffee.

"Wonderful," I said, but I didn't give it the same emphasis Clara had.

"They're staying a day or two in London before they bring their mother to Foxcroft," Clara said, "so you'll have some time to think about what you're going to say."

"I know what I'm going to say," I told her. "I'm going to be very proper and correct and say I'm glad to meet Nancy and I wish them happiness. Then I'm going to put on a cap and spend the rest of my life digging for Roman coins no one wants."

"I don't believe that for a moment, and neither do you." Clara laughed, and changed the subject. "Have you seen Charlie this morning? I think she was planning to give her dog a bath in honor of Wykeham's guests."

I rolled my eyes toward the ceiling. "She's probably in the kitchen splashing suds all over and causing the cook to give notice." I drained my cup. "I'll go find her. I need to get Griggins up here to help me with a new trench. He's probably helping Charlie."

I did find Griggins with Charlie, but in the stableyard, and poor Griggins was thoroughly drenched. I thought he had more suds and water on him than the dog did, but hated to say so. He was more than glad to turn the dog bath over to a stable boy so he could help me with my shovels and trowels.

Wykeham and Rebeckah stayed away for four days. Each day was a year long for me. I rehearsed and rejected a dozen plays in my head. I met Wykeham's mother and charmed her; I met his mother and she hated me. I met Nancy and she was beautiful and charming and I hated her; I met Nancy and she wasn't very beautiful and I hated her. I told Wykeham I loved him and he laughed at me; I told him I loved him and he told me he loved Nancy; I told him I loved him and he told me he loved me, too. During those days, I got absolutely nothing accomplished—I couldn't eat, I couldn't sleep. It was a terrible time. By the time Wykeham returned, I was thoroughly angry with him for putting me through such an ordeal. It was illogical and I knew it, but it was how I felt.

Wykeham presented himself at the door one fine afternoon just after I had returned from taking Annie to the vicarage for a lesson. He came in as if he hadn't been away at all. "I thought you might want to walk over and meet my mother," he said. I started to refuse, but was drowned out by Clara and Charlie saying "Yes!" The four of us and Charlie's dog started on the path to Foxcroft. Before long, the dog, Charlie, and Clara had walked ahead of us. I knew this wasn't the time or the place, but I had kept my feelings for four days, and I had to say something. I searched around for a subtle way to say what I wanted to. There was no way, so finally, I stopped abruptly in the path. "Wykeham, do you care for me?" I blurted.

He stopped and looked at me in surprise. "Of course. Why do you ask?"

"I mean, do you *care* for me?" I stumbled around for words. "Really *care*?"

He smiled at me, his eyes taking on a strange look. "You know I do."

It wasn't what I had wanted to hear. Had Nancy come to Foxcroft and reclaimed his heart? I bowed my head, bit my lip, and started walking along the path. He caught me by the elbow and stopped me. He put a finger under my chin and lifted my head until I was looking straight into his eyes. "And you, Frankie, do you care for me? Even a little?"

I started to say yes, then remembered Nancy. I knew I was making a complete fool of myself. I looked down, unable to meet his eyes, then took a deep breath. I didn't care anymore—I looked right into his eyes, feeling almost lost in them. "I love you," I said.

He looked slightly startled. "Would you say that again?"

"Wykeham, you aren't making this easy for me," I said. "I love you. Do you want me to shout it?"

"Yes," he said promptly, reaching to hold me.

"Don't. I'm not going to shout it," I said, almost crying as I turned away. I had told him how I felt, and he either hadn't believed me or he didn't care. *Nancy again*, I thought miserably. I wanted to die.

He ignored my protest, put his hands on both sides of my face, and forced me to look up at him. Then he bent and kissed me. It was the most wonderful feeling—I was flying, floating, soaring. When he lifted his head, my knees were weak.

"I'm glad you love me," he said with a touch of a smile, "because I've been in love with you for forever, it seems. I never thought you could care for me."

"You love me?" I couldn't believe my ears. "Why didn't you say something?"

"I couldn't, not with Harry always in the way. I wanted to, and I almost did once or twice." He brushed the side of my face with his lips. "I intend to tell you every day from now on."

"You love me?" I was in a daze. The world seemed to be spinning around me, and nothing was fixed except his face and his arms around me. Distantly I could hear Clara and Charlie coming back toward us. There was still something nagging at the corner of my mind. "Nancy," I said. "What about Nancy?"

"I love Nancy, too, but not as much as I love you," he said, bending to kiss me again.

I pulled away from him. "No, don't," I managed to gasp.

"Wait, Frankie, let me explain." Strangely, he was laughing at me.

I turned away. "No." I planned to say more, but Clara and Charlie came running up to us, along with Charlie's dog and another animal. This one was a large yellow hound that was quite the ugliest dog I had ever seen. It had one black ear and one brown ear, and its tongue was lolling out one side of its mouth. While Charlie's dog proceeded to jump up on Wykeham, the other animal made a dive right for me, its tongue swishing up the middle of my face.

"Do something!" I shrieked to Wykeham, but he was busy getting rid of Charlie's dog. I backed up to escape and wound up flat on my back with the dog standing on all fours over me, lapping at my face. Wykeham, just like a man, stood there and laughed at me.

"Get this thing off of me!" I yelled, putting my hands over my face to keep from being washed. "Go away!"

Wykeham grabbed the animal and pulled it away with a stern command. Then he knelt down and put his arms around me, helping me sit up. "You're all right, just a little worse for the wear," he said with a smile as he brushed my face with his fingers.

"Worse is hardly the word," I muttered. "Where did that repulsive animal come from?"

He laughed. "You're going to have to get accustomed to that repulsive animal when we're married," he said.

"Married?" Clara squealed. "How romantic! I knew you

two were made for each other. How very romantic! How wonderful!''

I stood shakily. "And what about Nancy?" I asked bitterly.

Clara looked at me strangely. "I suppose you'll just have to learn to get along with her. I'm sure you can do it."

"Never," I said. "How could you even think such a thing, Clara?"

Wykeham laughed and helped me to my feet. "I think it's time we sorted out this contretemps." He put a hand out to the dog, which immediately leaped up and rushed toward him. "Frankie, meet my best friend, Nancy," he said.

"Nancy?" I stared at the animal, which was now wagging its tail so hard that its whole body was shaking while its tongue lolled from the side of its mouth. "Wykeham, do you mean to tell me that you've let me think that Nancy was someone you cared about?"

"I do," he said promptly. "Nancy and I have had several adventures together."

"You know what I mean! Really, Wykeham, you led me to understand that Nancy was someone special in your life while this . . . this thing . . ." I couldn't go on. "I can't believe you could do this to me."

He put his arms around me. "I'm sorry, I truly am. You assumed Nancy was a woman, and I first thought it might make you jealous. After that, it suited my purpose. I thought since you had Harry, I could pretend a Nancy. It was just because I cared so much for you. Am I forgiven?" He touched my cheek and smiled down at me, his eyes warm with love. At that point, I would have forgiven him anything.

"Never. I mean, of course," I murmured, gazing up at him.

"Oh, how wonderful." I heard Clara speaking from far away. "How romantic! I knew it would happen this way— just like a perfect novel. Now would be the time when the hero would kiss her and sweep her off her feet."

And he did.